# ROCK THE BOAT

## THE BALLARD BROTHERS OF DARLING BAY, BOOK 3

## RACHAEL HERRON

HGA PUBLISHING

# OTHER BOOKS BY RACHAEL

Don't miss a minute in Darling Bay! **One unforgettable town, three standalone series (read them in any order!).** So many ways to fall in love!

**THE SONGBIRDS OF DARLING BAY:**
*Nashville meets the Gilmore Girls in this heartwarming new trilogy of estranged country-singing sisters seeking true love (and their way back to each other).*

The Darling Songbirds, Book 1
The Songbird's Call, Book 2
The Songbird's Home, Book 3

## THE FIREFIGHTERS OF DARLING BAY:

*Playing with fire has never been this fun...*
Blaze: Tox and Grace - Book 1
Burn: Coin and Lexie - Book 2
Flame: Hank and Samantha - Book 3
Heat: Caz and Bonnie - Book 4
Or get all four together on sale, HALF OFF! Save $5.97!
The Firefighters, Boxed Set

## THE BALLARD BROTHERS OF DARLING BAY:

*The Bachelor meets The Property Brothers: Love,*

property, and construction. What could possibly go wrong?

On the Market, Book 1
Build it Strong, Book 2
Rock the Boat, Book 3

## STANDALONE NOVELS:

*Women and families finding their ways back to what really matters: each other:*

The Ones Who Matter Most
Splinters of Light
Pack Up the Moon

## CYPRESS HOLLOW ROMANCES 1-5:

*Knit-lit with more heat than just wool could ever provide:*

How to Knit a Love Song

How to Knit a Heart Back Home
Wishes & Stitches
Cora's Heart
Fiona's Flame
Eliza's Home (Historical Novella)

## MEMOIR:

*Rachael's life as seen through the sweaters she's knitted:*

A Life in Stitches

## ON WRITING:

Fast-Draft Your Memoir: Write Your Life Story in 45 Hours
Onward, Writer!

## THRILLER (writing as RH Herron)

*"Mama, help me." A 9 1 1 dispatcher answers the phone, and it's her daughter on the other end of the line.*

Stolen Things

# ONE

The thing about Mrs. Donovan's boat was that it wasn't really a *boat*. Jake Ballard looked around and wiped his hands on the rag tucked into his tool belt. No navigation devices, no echo sounder. Nothing was even locked down. Mrs. D's boat was strictly live-aboard. He didn't think the *Sweetie Pie* had been sailed in the last three years even once, which should be a criminal infraction as far as he was concerned.

"That should do it," he said. "All fixed."

"What would I do without you?" Mrs. Donovan's voice was a purr.

Mrs. Donovan's stove went on the fritz on a regular basis, but instead of buying herself a new one (which she could probably afford, given the way she seemed to buy clothes), she preferred to call Jake on his cell at six in the morning, as she had that day. *It's broken again, honey. Can you come give this silly girl a hand?*

She wasn't a silly girl. She was a sixty-something widowed planner who enjoyed covering all her bases. When he'd arrived, she'd been wearing a silky red negligee and a matching robe. She fake-yawned him in, but her breath was minty when she kissed his cheek, and her eyelashes were startlingly perfect, long and black and curled so much they almost folded backward.

She'd lounged on the sofa and watched him work. Okay, she'd *ogled* him, watching him like the big yellow harbor cat watched for rats.

At least her stove seemed to legitimately be breaking down and not getting mysteriously unplugged like Maisie Dockett's electrical main. He'd already turned down Mrs. Donovan's offer of coffee, and of an English muffin, and if he didn't hurry, she'd offer him something worse, something she wouldn't like him to turn down.

"Yep, you should be all set." He lit a burner and watched it glow propane blue.

"Thank you *so* much, Jake." She undraped her person from the sofa and rose to kiss him (for the third time) on the cheek. "How can I ever repay you?" Her voice dripped honey.

"Maybe make me some of that banana bread?" Jake could admit he wasn't above accepting bribes of the non-sexual type, especially if the bribe landed on his doorstep and he could eat it alone in peace.

She pouted, pursing her bright red lips. "Is that all you want, really?"

He washed his hands briskly and dried them on the tail of his flannel shirt. "I sure do love what you do to a banana." He realized his mistake as soon as the words were out of his mouth. Her eyes lit with delight, and before she could utter a syllable, he sprang toward the stairs that led up and out to safety. "See you later! Okay! Bye!"

His boat was docked two slips away, and the deck was calling him, but instead of heading that way, he swung himself toward the marina store. He needed ice for his cooler since his brother Aidan was going to have him lay the flagstones at the Archer house today. He'd need a lot of ice-cold soda, and a huge sandwich, to boot. Maybe two apples. And some chips. Damn, maybe he *should* have accepted that English muffin Mrs. Donovan had offered him.

Jake gave a shout toward Ike who sat, as always, on his deck whittling a stick into a smaller stick. Ike never actually made anything, but he sure did like to carve non-things. He waggled his knife back in greeting and called, "Heard you're getting a new girlfriend!"

"It's just her stove," Jake said. "You know Mrs. Donovan."

"Not her, boy! The other one!"

Other what? Ah, it didn't matter. He walked on, still hungry and still very much not independently wealthy. That meant that he would have to go to work today instead of continuing to prep the *Kerplunk* for his trip to New Zealand, the trip he'd probably never be able to afford at the rate he was spending money on sandwiches at the marina store. He *really* needed to start making his own lunch, but Humphrey made the best turkey-cranberry sandwiches in the whole world.

"Yo, Jake! Enjoy your company later!" Justin, the owner of the fuel dock, hollered at him.

"What?" His company? It wasn't just his. It belonged to all three brothers.

Justin just laughed and threw a line around the cleat of a motorboat that chugged up to the fueling dock.

Jake yanked open the screen door of the bait shop. The tiny metal foghorn *whoo*ed over his head as the door slammed shut behind him. Darling Bait was a glorified bait and tackle shop that over the years had added things like deli sandwiches, ice cream, and greeting cards. As usual, Humphrey and

Bogart sat behind the cash register, Humphrey tying what must be his millionth fly and Bogart's long legs propped up on the glass counter. Bogart, of course, wasn't his real name. He was Steve Boggatini and didn't even work in the marina store. He was just best friends with Humphrey, the owner. This fact made everyone call him Bogart (or Bogey) at least seventy-five percent of the time. Humphrey was the direct opposite of Bogart, as plump and short as Bogart was tall and hale.

And both of them cracked the hell up when Jake walked in the door.

Yeah, something was up. "Okay," said Jake. "What's going on? Y'all planning a birthday party for me? Some kind of surprise to mark the occasion of my thirty-third journey around the sun?"

Humphrey shook his head, his heavy jowls wobbling as he did so. His grin stayed wide. "Sorry, son, didn't know about your birthday. When is it?"

"No time soon," he admitted. "I was just hoping. What's up around here? I can't walk five steps without hearing someone laugh, and I'm beginning to think it's because I have a hole in the backside of my jeans or something."

Bogart snorted. But he didn't add any information.

"Come on, guys."

Humphrey seemed to finally take pity on Jake.

He pushed the marina register across the counter and spun it so Jake could look at the page. "Looks like you got a new neighbor, son."

Jake scanned down the list of slips. There he was, number eighteen. Number nineteen had been open six months, ever since Lester and Sue headed out to the Panama Canal.

Now there was a name in the blank spot.

Mallory. His most recent ex, the one who had faked a positive pregnancy test. Yes, *faked*. First of all, they'd used protection. Second, the second red line had been wobbly and obviously done with a Sharpie. Third, which probably ought to have come first, she'd eventually admitted that she'd faked it.

Jake's head jerked up. "You're kidding me, right?"

Humphrey and Bogart roared with laughter.

"You can't let her."

"Hey, she requested it."

"She got a *boat*?"

Humphrey nodded. "You wanna know what she was going to name it?"

Jake groaned. "Probably not."

"I'm gonna tell you anyway!" He stabbed a finger into the air. "The *Future Mrs. Ballard!*"

Horror drenched him like a superheated wave. "Are you serious?"

Bogart collapsed on top of the counter, and

Humphrey slapped his leg so hard that it sounded like a firework popping off. "Nah, I just wanted to see your face. That was *worth* it."

"So she's not moving into nineteen?"

"Oh, yeah, she is. I made up the boat name, though. Probably something dumb like *Damsel in Distress*."

Bogart peeled himself off the counter, still snorting laughter.

"Hard no," said Jake. "You don't put exes next to each other."

"She has the cash, she has the boat. Where else was we gonna put her?" Humphrey rubbed the side of his nose, pressing one pink stub to another.

"Nope. Move me."

"We're out of free slips."

"Then I'll drop anchor in the bay and row my tender when I have to come in."

Humphrey said, "You'd do that? Just to avoid her?"

Bogart shook his head and said mildly, "I don't think she's that bad. I like the bagpipes."

Jake had almost forgotten that Mallory bonus. "She doesn't know *how* to play them. She just practices."

Bogart tipped his head. "Come on, son. Does *anyone* know how to play the bagpipes? You'd really anchor out there?"

What did it matter? Jake didn't like to get too settled anywhere anyway. He'd had enough of slip eighteen. Being out in the bay would be relaxing. Rowing the tender in would be...a pain in the ass, honestly. "Sure, I will. Then I won't even have to pay you rent."

"True," Humphrey said. "But you'll still need us. I know you still want your turkey/cran sandwich with extra mayo and no onions."

Jake longed to say, *You're wrong! I don't!* But he did, and he really hated onions.

He had to find a way out of his slip.

No, better, he had to find the money to finally get out of town and onto the open ocean, sooner rather than later.

---

BALLARD BROTHERS BUILDING and Realty was not only the realty office that Jake's oldest brother Liam ran, but also the headquarters for the three brothers' construction business.

Aidan, his middle brother, was already out in the metal shop, which was just what they called the large warehouse space at the back of the property. It was also the wood shop, and the storage area, and the planning office. Aidan ruled the domain with an iron and sometimes grumpy fist.

His brother shot Jake a look as he walked into the cramped front room that held a computer, a printer, and two extra sawhorses. "You're late."

Jake got to work every day just about the same time. "Maybe by three minutes, and that's not bad, seeing as how Mrs. Donovan waylaid me getting me to fix her stove again. And I've got to tell you, she's getting more blatant. I'm thinking I might need to start bringing a chaperone."

"Why don't you just start at the same time as the crew?"

"Why do we have to have this argument every day?" Jake liked to work on his boat before he got to the day job. Aidan knew that. It was a perk of being on the Ballard team.

That said, Jake, as the youngest, knew he was the one who got off easiest in terms of the family business. Liam sold houses, which sounded like a terrible job. Aidan managed getting the construction jobs as well as monitoring the crews, handling the master schedule, and dealing with the fallout when jobs ran over, as they inevitably did.

Jake just swung a hammer well. He also liked tiling and roofing, and he *really* liked running electrical, though he wasn't licensed yet. For the most part, he took directions calmly. He was good in a crisis.

And occasionally, he flaked the hell out and

didn't show up to work for three days because he got tangled in an existential *Must get out of town* mood. That usually meant sailing to the Farallons or farther. When that happened, his brothers covered for him.

It was a good job, though not one he wanted to get up even earlier for.

"So." Aidan slid into the wobbly green chair they "kept for clients," meaning Jake couldn't eat while sitting in it. He unrolled the Archer property plans. "I hear you're getting a new neighbor."

"Seriously?" Jake chomped into one of his two expensive apples. He spoke slowly around the juice. "So I really am the last to know."

"I just heard about it this morning from Molly at the diner," said Aidan. "So you're not happy about it?" Aidan wore a grin. He knew the answer.

"Dude. She was hook, line, and sinkering me. You know that!"

Aidan shrugged. "You got her to like boats."

Jake almost choked on a piece of apple. "Great?"

Aidan said, "Did you hear what she named it?"

Uh-oh.

Grinning, Aidan said, "*Night Moves.*"

"Oh, God."

"She did. Saw it getting painted in dry dock. In

pink, with a frilly little flourish next to an orange moon."

"I'm docking out in the bay."

"Even in winter? When it's freezing and windy?"

"I'll be gone by then."

"You *wish* you had the money to get out of here."

Jake sure as hell did. He chucked his apple core into the trash. "Still hungry."

Aidan jerked his chin. "Liam said he got some bagels. They're in the house. But hey, first we have to—"

Jake pointed at his torso as he spun toward the door. "Growing boy here. Be right back." As he walked toward the house, he realized he wasn't even that hungry anymore, which was a waste of a good morning appetite.

Women. He was just better off without them, honestly. He could ignore Mallory. He'd have to, and it wouldn't be that hard. No one since his first girlfriend, Zora, had ever gotten him tangled in the rigging, love-wise. And that was just fine by him.

# TWO

Zora paced back and forth on the front porch of Ballard Brothers Building and Realty. If she was lucky, they wouldn't hear her footsteps ringing hollow on the wood, and she could take a minute and talk herself out of the idea.

She didn't have enough money to buy a house.

Did she? She slid her hand in her bag and clutched the little book where she'd written down all the numbers: her savings, her puny retirement account, what little she had invested. Her eyes felt hot, and her heart beat too quickly.

The door opened. "Zora? Hey, there. I saw you out here—did you ring the bell?" Liam Ballard, neatly dressed in a blue suit, shook her hand.

"Sorry, no. Not yet."

"Come on in. Felicia's around somewhere. She might pop in to say hi."

Zora liked Liam's partner, but she was too nervous to think about making small talk. She should ask about their one-year-old baby girl, but the words got stuck in her mouth. She didn't see Jake, thank goodness. As she followed Liam into a cozy office in the front of the house, she said, "Do you really think I might have enough for a down payment?"

Liam's smile was meant to be comforting, she knew. "Like I said on the phone, let's see all your numbers, and then we'll be able to talk with a better idea of what we can make happen. Come on in. Sit."

Thirty minutes later, nerves flew up and down Zora's throat as Liam punched buttons on his computer. His face, always a kind one, stayed in the same position as he clicked his mouse rapidly. Neutrally interested. He hadn't seemed aghast at the amount she'd told him she had for a down payment.

She was trying not to talk—she really was. But God, it was hard. "It was a shock, you know?"

Liam made an *mmmm*-ing noise and kept staring at his screen.

"When Mom had to move into that residential living place. I honest to God thought she owned the house." For the last twenty years, Mom had been telling her that the house was their nest egg. *It's old and rickety, but when I'm old and sick, we'll sell it off so you can put me in a home and buy yourself a little house. Then you won't have to rent that place of yours anymore.* Zora had always thought it was morbid of her mother to say, but at the same time, it had never crossed her mind that Mom would have lied for that long. But Zora's mother hadn't owned even so much as a corner of the house. Zora felt so *dumb* about it all. Why hadn't she ever noticed that they'd never had to pay a property tax bill? Or home insurance?

"Mm-hmmm." Liam clicked some more keys, his eyes tracking back and forth across the screen. "Financially, it would have been easier for you now if you'd known you needed to save more."

Zora taught fourth grade. She saved as much as she could and ate Saltines with tuna many nights (she liked Saltines! Add a little arugula, and it was practically gourmet). "I know. I'm screwed. Any kind of house would be fine, though." Even a tiny one. The smallest, tiniest house would do.

He smiled kindly at her as he continued to cruise his fingers over the keyboard. "Just a few more minutes. Just trying to pull some strings here."

She'd been saving for years for a down payment, but her nest egg was still embarrassingly small. It wasn't as small as her mother's had been, though. Apparently Camille, Zora's mother, had gotten into some financial trouble years before when she'd had breast cancer for the first time, and she'd taken out a large mortgage, one she couldn't repay. Zora's mother had sold the house to her best friend, Davina Hill.

And Davina had let Camille live there, rent-free, ever since. It was a lovely thing to do. It was classy, and kind, and exactly the kind of thing Davina would do. It could have gone on forever, if Camille hadn't started falling so often that she needed assistance closer, necessitating the move to the care home.

Zora just wished that her mother had felt comfortable telling her the truth. Zora could have taken a second job, could have helped her mother buy back the house, leaving them more money for her care. Camille deserved better than the cheapest retirement home in town, but that's all Camille had been able to afford. She wouldn't let Zora touch her savings, no matter how much Zora insisted she didn't mind.

Was Liam's expression getting more downcast?

Desperately, she sent her gaze around the office. Two plaques from the city council, thanking the Ballard Brothers for their assistance in the community. Another three lauding Ballard Youth, their nonprofit. A picture of the three brothers standing with the Little League team they sponsored. Jake, of course, was the one her eyes were drawn to.

Crap. She babbled, "Mom said she just always thought she'd figure out a way to pay Davina back. Serves me right. No one should count on their parents to help with a down payment—it's not their parents' job." Zora just wished her mother hadn't told her so *often* that she would help. *Don't you worry about a thing, love. It'll all be taken care of, you won't have to worry about a thing.*

It *wasn't* all taken care of. Nope. Denny, her landlord, was going to sell her rental cottage—her heart ached at the thought—and she'd have nowhere to go. She couldn't afford the current rental market. She couldn't leave Darling Bay and her mother, but what the hell was she going to do?

Liam's lips got thinner as he stared at the screen. He was definitely not happy with what he was finding.

"Just tell me, Liam. Do I have enough?"

He turned carefully in his chair. "I'm sorry. You don't. I've run the numbers every way I can."

"Damn." Her fingers were so tightly clasped together they started to hurt.

"I've looked at every option. But this is a beach town in California, and everything's gone up since the recession."

Darling Bay was far enough north that it wasn't

quite a San Francisco bedroom community, but close enough that some tech people had built huge homes into the sea-facing hills. It was summer now, and as usual, the town filled with tourists. It was quaint, and everyone loved it, including Zora. "I should have known." She would *not* cry. Not now, in front of Liam.

"Hey, guys! What's up?" Jake Ballard. Of *course*. He held a bagel in one hand, a coffee in the other. With his height and broad, surfer shoulders, he looked—as usual—completely amazing. For a moment, Zora wanted to sink into the floor and never be seen again.

Zora stood, swallowing back a lump of tears and salt. "Thanks for trying, Liam, I appreciate it." Her words were fast, but her tongue felt thick.

Jake took another step into the office. "What are you two doing? You in the market, Zora?"

Good Lord, this was more than he'd said to her in years. Why, of all moments, was he talking to her now, when she was trying to get out without crying?

Liam said, "Stay, Zora. Sit back down. We can talk about other options—"

"No, I understand. I've got no options. I get it." She had *zero* options.

Ah, well. That was what happened when you got your hopes up, wasn't it? She should have known. Hopes got dashed, and you just had to keep on breathing and change your end goal. She knew that.

Jake held out a half of his bagel. "It's lox and cream cheese. Have it."

"Allergic," Zora said.

"To cream cheese?"

"Fish."

His jaw dropped, showing off the five-o'clock stubble he was sporting at nine in the morning. "You're allergic to *fish*? That's *terrible*."

"Mmm." Yeah, he'd actually said the same thing to her before, long ago, back when they dated. He'd probably forgotten all about that time. She hadn't.

In the hallway behind Jake, Felicia gave a wave. Oh, God. While Zora liked Felicia, she didn't so much want any more attention. She wanted her bed with its fluffy white duvet. She wanted to crawl in and pull the blanket over her head. She wanted to breathe hot, stuffy air until she started to pant from lack of oxygen. She wanted to be *alone*.

But Felicia moved quickly and gracefully, as always. She came in, kissing Jake smoothly on the cheek, Liam lightly on the lips, and then she hugged Zora. A cloud of light, flowery perfume trailed her, making the room seem as if it were filled with spring blooms. "How are you?"

Zora tugged her purse up her arm, pulling it tightly against her ribs. "I just got turned down for a loan, and then I turned down Jake's fishy bagel. Now I'm going to turn down the blankets on my bed." She couldn't believe she'd admitted that, and equally surprising was the fact that she could actually feel tears forming in her eyes.

Felicia gave her a strange up-and-down look. "Nonsense. Liam can make the numbers work. Can't you, my love?"

At the word *love*, Liam looked like he'd been hit by a magic wand. His eyes sparkled, and he turned to the computer with new vigor. "There *was* another first-time-homebuyer program..."

Zora sighed. A relationship like that must be nice. "Look, I get it, it's not necessary..."

"I'll just check a few more things. Hang tight."

Felicia's voice remained light. "Jake, can I talk to you about the show? With Aidan? He's in the metal shop."

Jake cleared his throat and wiped his mouth with a napkin. "Sure thing. Zora, good to see you."

It was weird, all of it. Jake didn't usually speak to her except for a *Hey* if they passed on the street. Sometimes it hurt, knowing that Jake Ballard still didn't like her, lo these many years after being high school sweethearts. It shouldn't bother her, but she had to admit that now and then it ached like a two-week-old bruise—just enough to be annoying. Jake seemed to get along with every single person in town. Everyone had a Jake-did-this-crazy-thing-once story. *Remember when me and Jake went bungee-jumping with the wrong kind of rope? Remember when me and Jake stopped up the waterfall?*

Zora's only story was that he'd broken her heart when they were just kids. "Yeah, you too, Jake."

He whistled his way out, and she remembered out of nowhere that they used to whistle for each other. His for her was a high *too-whee,* and hers for him was an upward swooping *whoo-hoot.* That had been fun, falling in love with him. It was good that she'd gotten over it.

She'd *totally* gotten over it.

It just wasn't that fun that he was seeing her on her lowest day in a long time.

Liam's brows furrowed into a deep frown as he punched more buttons.

There was no chance. She closed her eyes and prayed she could push the tears back behind them. She should have known better than to get her hopes up. Damn her mother and her empty reassurances. *You won't have to worry about a thing.*

Zora always had to worry.

# THREE

In front of Jake, Felicia walked briskly through the house and into the backyard. "Aidan's in a hurry this morning."

"I know. He already yelled at me about being late."

Over her shoulder, Felicia said, "I need both of your signatures for the new contracts. Hey, I heard you and Mallory are back together."

"You have *got* to be kidding me."

"Is it true you're sharing your boats or something? Tying them up together? Are you registered yet?"

Jake knew she was joking, but it honestly wasn't funny. He was sick of this town, sick of the people in it. He needed to be on the water, alone.

In the shop, Aidan said, "Good, you're back. I need you to run some boxes out to the Archers for me."

Jake shook his head. "I need a loan."

Aidan—damn him—laughed outright before saying firmly, "No."

Felicia said, "What for?"

Aidan didn't give Jake a chance to answer her. "He wants to leave. Take his boat and sail away and never come back."

"I'd come back. Eventually." Even as he said it, Jake wondered if it was true. He'd gotten happily lost out in the world before, and he'd always come back to where his brothers were, had always come back to Darling Bay. But what if this time it was different? What if New Zealand was the place where he'd finally want to put down roots? What *were* roots, anyway? Even growing up with Bill Ballard, the man who'd adopted and raised the three of them, Jake had mostly lived in the yard. Bill had converted the laundry room into a tiny room for him, just big enough to fit a twin-sized bed, but when Jake had said at nine that he preferred sleeping in a tent, Bill had just laughed and told him to go ahead.

Jake *had* preferred it. Freedom! At nine! Even then, he'd been more comfortable out of doors than in. Rootless, the way he liked it.

Aidan said, "How much?"

Jake named a number, a little lower than he'd actually need, but he had some savings from the last *On the Market* season.

Then both Felicia and Aidan laughed. Hard. The jackasses.

"Come *on*. I've got to get out of here. This town knows everything. The gossip is ridiculous."

"But you were fine yesterday." Aidan grinned annoyingly.

Aidan was wrong—Jake *hadn't* been fine the day before. At the Golden Spike Cafe, Molly had packed two orange muffins into a bag and handed him his mocha in a to-go cup. He'd been going to sit at the counter, and she hadn't even asked. She'd just assumed. Of course, he *had* been going to order a mocha and two orange muffins. But that aside, why did everyone in this town have to know absolutely everything about him?

"Do you ever stop to think about what it would be like to live somewhere else. Somewhere anonymous, where no one knows you?"

Felicia frowned. "It's awful. It's cold. It sucks to live in a place where even the guy at the convenience store can't remember your name." She'd come from L.A. to oversee the reality show that the Ballard Brothers starred in—*On the Market* was a cross between *The Property Brothers* and *The Bach-*

*elor.* Felicia had ended up being the first contestant to date a brother. That brother, Liam, had fallen for her, and therefore, Liam, the lucky dog, had only ever had to star in one episode before going *off* the market.

"But you can have *privacy* there. You know what it sounds like when Clancy starts getting it on with Mrs. Roobie? Did you know they both howl like cats? And he's four slips away! The first time I heard it, I almost called the cops." He regretted saying it as soon as it came out of his mouth. Now he was gossiping just like *them,* the rest of town. But then the thought hit him with a wallop. "Mallory *can't* dock in the slip next to me."

"When your boat's a'rockin', she'll come a'-knockin'?" Aidan tried to fist-bump him, but Jake didn't raise his hand to meet him.

Instead, he moved to sit on the edge of the rickety desk. "I've got to get out of here. How the hell am I going to get the money?"

Felicia whisked a folder out of her bag. "I'm glad you asked. I need your signature for the next show."

Jake groaned. Yes, being the only remaining bachelor of the Ballard Brothers was lucrative. The show paid bank. It paid double what he'd make in a year working construction for Aidan. But it still wouldn't be enough to fix his automatic radar piloting aid in time to leave for New Zealand this year. Plus, he still needed all the supplies.

On top of that, he *really* didn't want to do another show. Felicia waggled the pen at him.

"Is there any way out of this? Can't you break up with Liam? That guy's a jerk, honestly."

"Speak of the devil, and he arrives." Liam darted into the metal shop. "What are you guys—ah, it doesn't matter. Love, do you have the info on that lender that Carol used last year? I couldn't find it in the computer. Would it be in the cabinets out here?" He started to rummage through boxes full of paper that needed to be scanned.

"See?" said Jake. "He can't keep track of anything. Dump his ass."

Felicia shook her head. " If a man calls me love in front of his boorish brothers, I'm not putting him back on the show, if that's what you're asking. He's kind of a catch. He's good with the baby and let me sleep last night. In fact," she nudged Liam with her hip, "I just saw you being really nice to some woman crying in your office."

Jake's throat clenched. "Zora was *crying*?" How had he not noticed that?

Liam nodded briefly and kept rummaging. "Turns out her mom didn't own that house she's been living in for the last twenty years. Her mother just moved into that retirement care place on

Maple, the one with the separate tiny apartments, and her mom's money has to go to that. Zora just doesn't have enough saved for a down payment unless we find her some free cash somewhere."

The idea of Zora crying made Jake want to punch someone, and he generally didn't resort to violence. The stupid eighteen-year-old heart that was apparently still beating in his chest made him want to give her the money he'd squirreled away. For a crazy split second, he imagined handing it over to her in a suitcase. Or better, leaving it on her doorstep and watching from a distance as she opened it.

Ha. Like he'd forget the sailboat, forget his dreams.

Nope.

So his first girlfriend still tugged at his heart a tiny bit. He'd been over her for more than a decade. "Look at this! *This* is how this town gossips. You think Zora would want us to be talking about her state of financial affairs? You think she'd be happy with that? God, we suck." He grabbed the pen from Felicia's fingers and signed the show papers at each Post-it flag.

"You're right. I'm being a dick." Liam looked chagrined, his lips pulled tight. "I shouldn't talk about it to you guys. But honestly, with as little as she makes as a fourth-grade teacher, I'm completely shocked she can even afford to rent a place in town. She doesn't even have much in retirement."

Jake couldn't help saying their adopted father's phrase, "Broke as a drunken gambler riding home in the morning, huh?"

From outside, next to the open doorway, came a voice Jake could conjure without even trying.

"*Pardon* me?"

# FOUR

Zora felt heat sweep her body from the scalp down. "What the hell, Liam?" Jake's comment was ugly and painful, but Liam was supposed to be her realtor.

Liam turned with his palms turned toward her. "Zora. This *isn't* how I usually talk about my clients. I was just looking for that FHA packet. I apologize."

"Not cool." She took a breath and tried to extinguish the flames spreading inside her chest. "Super uncool." What a dumb way to say that she was upset.

"I'm really sorry," said Jake simply. Then he went back to signing papers that Felicia was flipping for him. His cheeks were as red as hers felt. Maybe he was embarrassed. Good.

Liam was gabbling words. "Here we go. I found what I was looking for. A long shot, of course. But I'm going to—oh, yeah. We can get this done. Or we can do something. Hopefully. I know that—oh. Let's get back to my office, and we'll go over your options."

"My very limited options with my very limited down payment." She tried to sound amused, but the words came out bitter instead. Funny, she didn't feel bitter. She felt sad, right down to the soles of her feet.

And scared.

There was no way Denny, her landlord, would let her keep paying so far below market rate for much longer, not now that the rates had skyrocketed. He kept saying he was going to sell. She'd gotten in cheap because he'd been doing construction on the place. She'd lived in it *while* he'd had half the foundation lifted and stabilized. She got used to living around rubble and the sound of hammering. Now, even though it could still use some work, her little cottage was perfect for her. She'd lived there long enough to bring the old garden back into life, as well as the school garden just on the other side of the fence.

She'd *had* a plan. She would stay in the perfect

rental cottage as long as Denny would let her, hopefully until she and Mom decided to sell the house. Then she would buy a sweet little home in Darling Bay and build her mother the tiny house she'd always wanted. Zora would live alone, of course. Always alone. Even when Zora dated, she'd never considered making the mistake of moving in with a boyfriend or having one move in with her. Hell, no. Too much risk.

Liam waved his hands like he was conducting an unruly band. "We'll find something—there's got to be something I haven't thought of—"

Felicia stepped forward, leaving Jake to turn his own pages. "Don't bother, darling. I've just had the most wonderful idea."

"Sorry?" Poor Liam was sweating.

"Zora, how much do you have?"

For some reason, she answered her honestly. "I have twenty-two thousand saved." It was a number she'd thought was huge. But as a twenty-percent down payment, it would apparently only buy her a chicken coop in this beach town. A coop that leaned.

"Honey," Felicia turned to Liam, "What if she had triple that? Would she be able to get a place she could afford the mortgage on?"

"Yeah, but—"

"Fantastic. Zora, sweetie, are you dating anyone?"

Zora's skin went cold. At the same moment, Jake looked up from his paperwork and met her eyes. That deep blue, like the ocean—she'd almost forgotten the color of his eyes.

"Zora?"

She turned to Felicia, fervently wishing she could say, *Yes, actually, I'm engaged.* It was a wish she'd never had until this very moment. But she wasn't good at lying, and in this town, they'd all know she was doing it, anyway. "No. Not right now."

"You *have* to be our next homebuyer for *On the Market.* Do you know the show?"

How could she not? Every season, a woman shopped for, bought, and renovated a house while dating a Ballard brother as the work was going on. The whole damn town celebrated with everything but a parade each time a season was released. The Golden Spike saloon played them back to back the day they came out, and the season finale was always shown to a packed house. Or at least, that was what she'd heard. So many people packed into the bar made her nervous, even when the fire marshal was on the scene, and she preferred to binge it all at home. Especially since Jake had been the only brother dating for the last three seasons.

"I, um, know the show." She'd thought of it as *The Jake Show*. Her own private, personal wallowing ground. Super fun.

No, scratch that. She didn't *wallow* when it came to Jake. She'd been over him for years. It was just nice to watch his muscular body install beadboard. And sweat in the sun on top of roofs. And laugh with his brothers on the deck of his boat as the sun went down.

"We'll give you forty thousand to be on the show. Free and clear. You'll have sixty-two thousand to use for a down payment."

This was crazy. The words scraped out of her throat. "No, thanks. I'm good."

Felicia's voice was a purr. She was right next to Zora now, a light hand on her shoulder. She smelled of flowers, expensive ones. "Think about it. A house of your own. A down payment that you wouldn't have to pay back, ever."

Zora felt a little woozy. "No. I think...no, thank you." She couldn't date Jake Ballard on air. Not after she'd watched him on her TV screen date Iris and Jacklyn and Keala. Every time the cameras had zoomed in on one of those other women kissing him, Zora had felt a giddy nostalgia and a heady rush of desire. She wasn't going to feel that way in front of the nation.

Nothing could possibly sound worse to her.

"Or you could put the money you've saved toward helping your mother and just use the forty as a down?" Felicia's voice was velvety.

Zora's heart clutched. "We'll be okay."

"But you're *perfect*. I mean, look at you." Felicia had somehow taken both Zora's hands and stepped backward, looking her up and down. "You're cute as a button. Your figure is to *die* for."

Zora blinked. She had curves, that was all. Curves that would show as heavy on screen, right? Wasn't that what they said, the camera added ten pounds? It would look like more on her.

"And this face! It's angelic. Don't you think, Jake?"

Jesus Christ on a swizzle stick. "Please stop." But she glanced at him. He looked frozen in place, a statue—no, like someone on a starting line, waiting for the gun to tell him to run. This was *so* much more awkward than the dozens of times over the years that they'd had to spend time together with mutual friends at the bowling alley, the bar, the cafe.

"Come on," said Felicia. "This is too good to let go. You get everything you want, and the only thing you have to do is go on a couple of dates with this guy."

*This guy.*

This guy was the problem. Of all people in the

world. She'd rather date a Fox News host. Jake was unsafe for her in so many ways.

"Hey, but what do I get out of it?" Jake had recovered and wore that patented half-grin on his face.

Aidan didn't look amused. "Um, your part of the share of the show money?"

"And a bonus." He kept his eyes on Felicia—he didn't glance in Zora's direction.

Her cheeks flared. He needed a *bonus* to date her. "This whole thing is a terrible idea."

But no one seemed to be listening to her.

Jake rapped the edge of the desk. "Think about it. This isn't fair. I have to do all the work, you know?"

That pushed Zora right over the edge into defending the dumb idea. "Isn't *fair*? All the *work*? It would be that terrible, going out on two fake dates? Jesus, Jake, you're a real piece of—"

Felicia said, "No, that's not what he means—"

Jake interrupted, "Not her specifically, but the whole idea of it."

*Her.* He couldn't even say her name. It was funny. In town, people thought they were friends. Something about everyone knowing that they'd dated in high school combined with everyone knowing and loving Jake meant that they sent him messages through her sometimes. *If you see Jake, tell him thanks for bringing in my mail while I was gone. Hey, if you run into Jake, tell him I've got that money I owe him.*

But she and Jake hadn't had a real conversation in more than a dozen years.

Jake touched her elbow, and static snapped between them. She jumped backward, swallowing her yelp. He went on, not seeming to notice. "I'm the only Ballard who's single. The show is based on the fact that one of us dates the eligible bachelorette."

Was *that* what she'd be?

"And I'm the only who can do it since you two are in *love* and have *principles*." He put the words in air quotes.

Zora opened her mouth to say something—anything—but he spoke first.

"So I need the show to double my part of the take."

Zora and Felicia both gasped, for obviously different reasons. Zora said, "You need *double* to go out with me?"

"Double?" said Felicia. "That's a lot."

"Bull. Sorry, Zora, it's not you." His gaze flashed quickly to her and then away again. "But Felicia, you just gave her forty thousand without even blinking. You know the show has the money."

"It's not fair to your brothers, though. The payments have always been split into thirds. Honey?" Felicia turned to Liam.

Aidan and Liam shared a glance and then both shrugged. Liam said, "As long as we get the same amount as we always have, why would we care? And he's not wrong. He does have to do all the work. We just do what we normally do—I sell houses, and Aidan fixes them. Jake's got to do everything else."

Aidan snorted. "And he does 'em, all right."

Zora felt queasy. She couldn't do this. She couldn't go on national television and date her ex who had actually been filmed coming out of the last contestant's bedroom wearing nothing but a towel and a smile, especially when he would obviously rather chew light bulbs than have her be the homebuyer.

That last word, though.

*Homebuyer.*

If she did this, she'd be able to buy a house. Her perfect house, the one she'd *make* perfect and hopefully stay in, safe and snug, until she died cheerfully alone in happy old age.

She'd have a *home*.

"Fine," Felicia said with a sigh. "I'll talk them into it. If you three are sure."

All three brothers nodded.

"And Zora? Are you in? Should I get the paper-work printed?"

A word—she wasn't sure which one—got stuck in her throat.

"Zora?"

A house. A home. *Her* house. *Her* home. "I need a day to think about it."

Felicia frowned but said, "Okay. But by tomorrow noon, latest."

# FIVE

At the Archer site, Jake helped Gabriel Costa lay in electrical to the sunporch addition. Jake had protested at first, wanting just to hammer something. Anything.

But Gabriel said, "Come on, man, you're good at this. Thought you'd be grateful I want you to help me and not Bass. You like the electrical. He likes it, too, but he's gonna kill himself one day."

Jake did like wiring work. Normally. He hadn't liked it when that static shock had snapped between his hand and Zora's elbow. "Yeah, I know."

Halfway through the job, he couldn't help himself. "Hey, what *is* static, anyway? How does it build up?"

Gabriel handed him a level to hold. "Huh?"

"You know, when you touch a car door. Or someone else. And that static snaps."

"It means you need a dryer sheet."

"I hate those things."

"Oh, yeah, I forgot you're a hippie who dries his T-shirts on a clothesline on his boat."

"They smell good that way. And the sun's free. Everyone wins."

Gabriel pointed. "Hand me that wrench. Thanks. I dunno, my old lady and me got that."

"The static?"

He nodded. "Always have. Ever since the start. If I don't see her all day, it kind of builds up. Sometimes she licks her fingers so that it doesn't happen, but we still kind of get a jolt. You ever get the hit on your lips? It hurts. But in a good way. Why you ask?"

Should he lie? No, Gabriel was a good friend, and Jake wasn't that great at lying. "I got a big jolt when I shook hands with the new potential contestant."

Gabriel sat back on his heels and straightened, massaging his lower back. "No shit. That's a good sign, huh? What's she look like?"

All of the women who'd been on the show so far had been imported to Darling Bay from the outside world. Zora would be the first local. "She's pretty. Looks a lot like my high-school girlfriend, actually."

"Like Zora? That's a good look, I guess, if you like short and curvy and a little boring."

Startled, Jake said, "Boring?"

"You know. Brown hair, brown eyes, just kind of medium everything. Cute lips, I noticed that. But she's always nervous and twitchy, like a mouse. Like she's about to run away in a minute, you know?"

He knew the running-away look, but he didn't know about the medium part. Zora's eyes weren't medium—they were deep, dark pools, the kind a man might not be able to swim out of. Zora's hair was thick and dark, falling in natural waves past her shoulders. She'd had a streak of white at her temple since her early twenties, and it was grown out now, running all the way through her hair.

"And that hair," said Gabriel. "Kind of *bruja*, right? Like she's got kids locked in a gingerbread house somewhere."

"If by 'witch,' you mean gorgeous."

"Oh, shit. It's *her*?"

Gabriel had always been smart.

"Yeah," Jake admitted.

"*Dio.* That gonna fuck you up?"

"Of course not. That's so far in the past I can barely remember what happened." *Liar.* He remembered everything. Especially the way she'd hurt him.

"And she snapped you? That static?"

Jake nodded.

Gabriel whistled. "You're screwed, my friend."

"I know."

"Don't get your heart twisted, you hear me? Unless you're ready to settle down."

"Settle *down?* This is me you're talking to!" Jake thumped his chest, feeling like an idiot as he did so. "Do I *ever* get my heart broken? Ever?" He was legendary among the work crew. Love 'em and leave 'em wanting more.

Yeah, that worked out well. See item number one: Mallory moving her boat next to his. But still... "My heart doesn't twist."

"Famous last words, bro. Famous last fucking words."

## SIX

"Don't put those so close to the microwave. I don't want them radiated."

Zora moved the tomatoes nearer to the sink. "I don't think that's how it works, Mom."

Camille shook her head as she brushed her long silver hair over her shoulder. "I read about it online. You nuke everything when you use that thing, everything that's in it and everything that's not, too."

"How far does the exposure go?"

"Miles." Her mother settled further into her recliner and settled her pink fleece around her shoulders.

"So does that mean that we're all getting irradiated by everyone's microwave in this whole facility? Right now?" Each unit was tiny, and everything in each apartment was cheap, so it *was* possible that the microwave wasn't the best quality.

"It sure does mean that."

"Then why do I have to move the tomatoes?"

"Don't get smart. Now, look at this. Did you know this recliner has heat? Did you ever hear of such a thing? I can move it up and down, and even get it to put me in a standing position." Her mother pressed the buttons and rode the chair from sitting to standing and then back down. "This is the best thing in this place, I swear to God."

Zora put the lettuce in the crisper. "Don't get stuck in it like you did the bathtub."

"That was an accident. Did you wash that lettuce?"

"Twice," Zora said.

"And dried it?"

"Dry as a bone."

"Because you know that if you don't dry it, it gets mold. Mold can kill you twice as quick as salmonella."

Zora nodded as she reached for a knife to slice the enchilada she'd just reheated. "So you like the recliner, at least. That's a good thing."

"I do. Even though someone died in it."

The knife slipped, and Zora almost nicked her forefinger. "Pardon?"

"It's true. The woman in here before me died in this very chair. Just gave up breathing, her ass right where mine is."

"Who told you that?"

"Evelyn in 119."

"Do you think she was telling the truth?"

Camille fiddled with the remote. "An old man said he'd heard that, too. John. Or Larry. I can't tell any of them apart. They all look the same. Old."

Zora's mother had had her late in life, a surprise at almost forty. Zora had never known her father, and that was fine by her—he'd been a passerby going through town, and Camille had always been enough mother and father for her. Now, at seventy-three, Camille was one of the younger residents in the home. "Okay, then. Are you all right with that? We can get you a new chair if you want."

With a shrug, Camille batted the idea away. "I asked the house manager, and she told me that the old lady didn't even release her bowels when she died. So I'm fine with it."

"Oh, my God."

"Think about it. This building's been here for a long time, right? The only way this apartment turns over is when someone kicks the bucket. It's not like they get a new job and move to Ohio. I figure someone's died just about everywhere in here. Glad I brought my own bed." *Zzzzzzzt.* Camille's recliner carried her into a prone position so that she was staring up at the ceiling. "If I'm lucky, I'll topple over into the pool. They've only ever had one person die in it, and it was a man. I'd be the first woman to die out there."

"Mom! Cut it out!" How many times had Zora listened to her mother speculate about her own death? A thousand? More? And yet Camille always found a new and shocking way to make Zora imagine her demise. "You told me you liked it here." She gave her mother the heated enchilada. Meals came with the lodging, but Camille complained about the bland stews. She preferred microwaved Mexican.

"I did not say I liked it here," snapped Camille. "I'd never say that. I only like this chair."

Time for a subject change. "You'll never guess what happened today."

"You met a man."

"I don't need a man." It was a kneejerk answer, something she said to her mother every time they saw each other. "Do you ever watch *On the Market?*"

A smile stretched across Camille's face. "Oh, *yes.* It's wonderful. Why do you ask? I thought you didn't watch that show."

Crap, what was she thinking? For a second, she'd been seriously thinking about telling Camille what had happened, that she'd gone into the realty office to see about getting a loan and had been rejected. It would have brought up all over again her mother's shame about not being able to help Zora with a house of her own. That shame was ridiculous. Her mother had raised her and had loved her. She owed Zora nothing. "Someone was...someone was talking in town about it, and I was wondering if you still followed it."

"Wouldn't it be something if we could get you on there?"

Zora changed her mind. It wasn't the right time to tell her mother they'd offered her a place on the show. "That would just be silly."

"You'd get to date Jake! Again!"

Zora stared in astonishment. Her mother had hated Jake for what had happened to her. She'd literally called him the devil. "Wait. What?"

"He's so handsome!"

"Who are you?"

"Evelyn in 119 has me meditating. I think it's scrambled my brain a little, but I sure feel good."

Zora smiled. "Really? So you're ready to let go of things you've held onto for years?"

Camille's eyes shone bright. "Remember when

Junior's Burgers tried to kill me by giving me sal-monella?"

"I remember. That was the spinach, and it got people all over the state. It wasn't their fault." Her mother had always blamed Junior and made the sign of the cross whenever they passed the restaurant.

Camille nodded. "I know. I ordered pizza from them the other night. With spinach!"

"Wow. Also, spinach on pizza is weird."

"It's not! Evelyn in 119 told me about it! It's delicious."

"Your BFF is full of advice."

"And now I don't hate Jake. You both were just kids. You should give that guy another shot."

This was too much. Camille had always been so overly protective—it was like the sea turning into a meadow. Her not hating Jake—worse, encouraging her to give him a chance? Zora felt shaken to her core.

So she reached for her purse. "Speaking of spinach, I've got to get some groceries on the way home."

"Have an enchilada! I'm not even done eating! You're going to make me wash my dish all on my own?"

Her mother was only mostly teasing. She had a perfectly good dishwasher, the newest appliance in the apartment. Feeling like an asshole but unable to stop herself, Zora dropped a kiss on her mother's head.

*Dating Jake to get a home of her own.*

Zora needed to be inside her current home, tucked in bed and safe, before she could start really thinking about it. And so she fled.

SEVEN

At home, Zora let out Mr. Prickles, her Siamese, who liked to roam the garden late at night. It wasn't the best deal—he always started crying at two in the morning outside her window, demanding to be let back in, but it was worse if she didn't let him out at all.

Zora poured herself a glass of wine and took it and the mail out to the back porch. Mr. Prickles had it right, at least. The garden was the best part of the rental house. As the cat swatted at invisible things underneath the jasmine, Zora watered the porch plants. She'd put the lower vegetable garden on a drip system that she'd set up herself. She loved her garden. But the very, very, *very* best part of the garden was the part on the other side of the back gate.

Her garden abutted the back corner of Darling Bay Elementary, where she taught. The administration had let her start a small community garden with her fourth-grade class. Each year in September, they took over where the last class had left off. Just on the other side of her fence, chard and onions and kale grew on school grounds through the winter. The local coffee shops gave them their grounds for the compost pile. When the garden was blooming, full of tomatoes and lettuce and sugar peas and cucumbers, each student got to take a turn taking home a salad for their family.

Her kids loved it. And more than anything else, she loved watching them in the raised beds, hooting over worms and drawing straws to see who got to turn the compost pile.

The fog had settled over Darling Bay, its summer blanket, and while it cooled the air, the stored heat of the day rose up from the earth as she watered. Jake's image floated into her mind, his broad jaw, the way his neck was muscled, and how his shoulders filled his T-shirt.

The idea of dating him in order to move... Her chest heated.

No, this current rental was heaven. Why would she want to leave? Why would she *want* to move, to buy a house, anyway? Maybe Denny would forget about selling. Maybe he'd want to hold onto it longer, to build more equity.

It was a sign, the fact that she didn't have enough money saved yet. Maybe when she did, the perfect house would materialize, and she'd be able to consider moving away from this garden. Of course, by then, house prices would have skyrocketed in the coastal town even more than they already had, and she'd probably never be able to afford to get into the market. Not on a teacher's salary.

Maybe she *should* get a second job. But doing what? They didn't even have Uber in Darling Bay. They had Ernest, who drove his battered taxi around on Friday and Saturday nights (the car always smelled strongly of weed, which made most people call their friends or neighbors for rides instead). Could she be a one-woman rideshare? Her car was old and beat up. So maybe not the best idea.

Zora turned off the hose and went inside, just as her phone pinged.

*Hey.*

It was Tuesday. She and Tuesday taught at the same school—Tuesday had second grade and wore cute tunics which, with their big pockets, came in handy in her classroom (once she'd emptied them to show Zora: they were full of drawings of frogs and broken crayons and kids' used Kleenex).

Tuesday was sweet and fun and one of Zora's best friends.

She was also Aidan Ballard's girlfriend. She'd been on the show a few years before.

Zora shouldn't text back. Should she?

Then she did: *I'm freaking out.*

*Time to buy a house?*

Of course Aidan would have told her the show had been offered to her.

*I can't.*

*Then what the heck are you going to do?*

To do? At some point Denny *would* up her rent or kick her out. Rental pricing had gone up, she knew, to the rate of a hefty mortgage payment. And it was only going to get worse.

*Move to Eureka?*

*Over my dead body. I can't teach without you.*

Zora loved Tuesday for her bravery. *Yeah, right. You wouldn't even notice I was gone.*

*Take the show's offer.*

The phone sat in Zora's hands, glaring blue light at her. From the back porch came a yowl that sounded like Mr. Prickles was dying. When she rushed to the door, though, he was merely tussling with a moth almost as big as his head. "Damn you, cat."

She sat back on the couch. The screen had gone to sleep, but she could still see the words burned into her retinas: Take the show's offer.

She texted back, *Then I'd have to date Jake.*

*So what? You're old news.*

*We made each other sad.* Or maybe it had just been him who made *her* sad. Who was to say that he was even affected?

*You were kids. I don't even remember the name of the first guy who broke my heart, though I sure remember other things about him pretty clearly...*

Zora shot her a smiley face with heart eyes.

*And HEY. I know you. You're no dummy. You're thinking about it!*

Zora paused before tapping. *Maybe.*

The phone rang in her hands.

Zora didn't even bother to say hello. "I'm not going to do it."

"You're killing me. Why not?"

"Because." She should have poured herself another glass of wine, but then she would get even more maudlin later. She poured a large glass of water, instead, and stood in the kitchen, leaning against the countertop, gazing at the sink. That blasted faucet had broken last year, and instead of asking Denny to send Vinay the plumber out, she'd watched videos on YouTube and learned how to fix it herself. It still sprayed slightly to the left, but she didn't care.

"Great reasoning," said Tuesday. "I can get behind 'because.'"

"Come on. I just can't."

"They basically offered you a house, and you turned them down. If you get a small place, your mortgage won't be much higher than your rent is now. That's balls-ass dumb, I hate to break that to you. What possible reason did you give them?"

"I just said no and ran."

"Meant with love, but...*typical.*"

Heat rose in Zora's chest. "Hey."

"No," said Tuesday bluntly. "You don't pay attention to the things that are right around you. You always thought you'd get money from your mom's house, but you didn't bother double-checking."

It felt terrible to be reminded that she'd thought that way, but it was true.

Tuesday continued, "You can't afford to buy a house without bigger savings. You're going to be priced out of the market in about ten minutes. You get offered a free down payment double what you've saved? What does the universe have to do to get your attention? Give you a blow job and a pony?"

"You're right." Zora only whispered the words,

but they were loud enough for Tuesday to catch. Of course.

"I *am*. Now. Do you want me to meet you at the Ballard Brothers' office tomorrow morning or tomorrow afternoon? Personally, I think morning is better."

Zora felt sick to her stomach. "Oh, my God. What if they find someone else? Of course they will. Have you seen the women they get? They're gorgeous. Tall. Thin. Funny. Usually rich enough to buy a house in Darling Bay. They buy *nice* houses. Ones with views."

"Hello. I'm neither tall nor thin nor rich, though I *am* funny as hell."

"Sorry." Zora changed her mind and poured a second glass of wine. "You're going to be responsible for my hangover tomorrow."

"You think you don't deserve it."

"I will totally deserve a hangover."

"Not that. You think you don't deserve a nice home."

"Deserve? It's not about that! It's about what I can afford."

"Is it?"

"What do you mean?"

"I mean, you're always scared to do anything, and I think it comes down to that you don't believe you're worthy enough to take big risks for yourself."

Zora walked into the tiny bedroom. She'd painted the walls a deep red and hung gold-framed prints of yellow dahlias on the walls. She set the wine on her nightstand and fell backward onto her bed with a thump. "That's not even fair. I should hang up on you, you jerk."

"I love you, too." Tuesday took a long, audible breath. "Honey, take the risk. You'll forget you're on camera in about an hour. It's not as hard as it seems like it'll be. It's summer vacation. There couldn't be a better time—you don't even have to take time off. What are you going to do now?"

"I don't know." She didn't. She shouldn't have to make up her mind this fast. Instead, she needed a few hours and a big pad of paper. She could weigh the pros and cons and list the benefits next to the drawbacks.

"Zora, I can *see* you in my mind. You want to reach for a pen and paper, but screw that. For once in your life, you're being handed an opportunity coupled with a full down payment. On the same day. I know you're scared of everything, but girl, you have *got* to pull up your big girl panties."

Zora groaned. "You know I hate that phrase."

"That's why I used it. What are you going to do?" she asked again.

"I don't know."

"What are you going to *do*?"

"I'm telling you, I don't know."

Tuesday was a broken record. "What are you going to do?"

"Do you think I can stall?" There were complicating factors. But she couldn't talk to Tuesday about what had really happened back then.

"No."

"Damn it, Tuesday."

"Just jump."

"Don't say it."

"Leap, and the net will appear."

"Thank you, Inspirational Poster, for the pep talk." Zora pulled her buckwheat pillow alongside her body and leaned on it.

*Jake.*

He was the real reason, the reason she couldn't tell Tuesday why she was hesitating, of course. Jake had proven himself unsafe for her to be around, and it had broken Zora inside.

Could she face that again? Being around him, being always reminded of what had gone wrong?

"Zora, you're braver than you think you are. You're braver than you feel right now."

Jake had broken her.

But he couldn't break her twice, could he?

"Fine. I'll do it."

A crow of delight came over the receiver. "Oh, my God, I can't believe it!"

Neither could Zora. This might end up being a decision she regretted for the rest of her life.

But, hell, she'd survived that once already, and it had only nearly killed her.

Literally.

# EIGHT

Jake slumped lower in Liam's fancy stretchy-fabric chair as Felicia used the mouse to flick through profiles. His head ached from not being able to sleep the night before. Irritation with Mallory, who'd, sure enough, chugged her new sailboat into the slip next to him, vied with the strange disappointment that Zora hadn't immediately agreed to be on the show the day before.

"Look at her. She's pretty, right?" Felicia pointed at the stunning blonde on the screen.

"Yep." Typical Beach Barbie, the kind that flocked from SoCal to their colder coastline and complained about the fog and the rocky beaches.

"You like her? Yeah?"

"Nope."

Felicia didn't seem to mind at all. She kept clicking. "What about this one?"

Jake made a noncommittal noise. *Why* had Zora said no? Okay, she hadn't said no, but she hadn't said yes, and now Felicia was walking him through a backup plan.

It was a huge sum of free money, but Zora had effectively said that not taking it might be better than spending any time at all with him. It wasn't as if on the show they had to spend *that* much time in each other's company. In the last season, he'd gone on two short dates with Joy and worked on the house with her a couple of times on camera. Couldn't have added up to more than eight hours, all told.

So Zora couldn't be paid forty thousand to spend even one single workday with him.

It wasn't like they'd never hung out with each other since high school, either. This was Darling Bay. Of course they'd ended up at the same crab feeds and birthday parties. Just last year, they'd been at the saloon when Dust & Rusty were playing. He'd seen her on the dance floor with old Gus Treat. Her pale blue dress had swung when she twirled, her smile lighting up the rafters above their heads. He'd wondered why they'd never hooked up as adults. He'd cut in on the dance. She'd smiled, and they'd talked about something light for the second half of the song. Then she'd disappeared into the crowd.

He'd thought they were fine. He'd always thought that, ever since he got over his broken heart (which, admittedly had taken longer than it should have, but he'd been eighteen. Everything had felt worse than it actually was).

What if they'd never been fine? What if she *hadn't* wanted to dance with him when he cut in? What if she'd done that polite-woman thing and grinned and bore it till it was over? What a dick he would be if he hadn't noticed that.

He probably hadn't noticed.

Felicia nudged him in the side. "How do you feel about brunettes?"

He thought of Zora's hair, dark brown with its white stripe. "I like 'em. Hey, how do you know if someone dislikes you?"

She looked surprised but said, "Well, no one dislikes me, so I don't actually know. You, on the other hand..." She trailed off with a smile. "Oh, you're serious. Okay. I think you just know, don't you?"

Obviously he didn't know, or he wouldn't be asking. He shook his head.

"All right, you socially clueless weirdo, I guess there are two ways you can know. First one is they tell you, which is the way I prefer it. Or they're consistently rude to you. The flip side is if they don't really like confrontation, then they can just avoid you."

"For how long?"

Felicia tilted her head. "As long as possible, I guess. Maybe you see them at a party, but when you get to where you last saw them, they're gone."

Zora at Lily Dario's fortieth birthday party.

"Or maybe you have a lot of friends in common, but you never seem to hang out together as a group."

Zora was friends with everyone in his friend group. But he hadn't spent time with her, even in a group, for years. "Huh." He'd avoided her right after the breakup, sure. But after he got home from college, he hadn't really thought to. They'd dated, she'd broken his heart for the first time, he'd gotten over it and moved on.

Or at least he thought he had. But knowing this —finding out that she actively disliked him? Somehow that hurt way more than it should have.

"Are you thinking of anyone in particular?"

Jake shook his head again. "Nah. Course not."

"Not Zora?"

"Zora! Why her?" Seeing motion in the corner of his eye, he glanced out to the porch. "Zora! Jesus Christ!"

"What the hell?" Felicia looked startled at his shout.

Jake sprung out of the chair. "She's here!" It was like he'd conjured her. "She's here!"

She patted his arm. "It's okay. This could be good. I'll go let her in."

Jake felt frozen, his feet iced to the floor. Suddenly he knew very seriously that maybe it was *not* okay between them. Yesterday, he'd kind of thought it might be fun to have a fling with his first girlfriend (his first of many). He'd always held a special place in his heart for her. When he saw her in town, he'd always felt a certain glow of warmth toward her.

But she hadn't been feeling the same thing. She actively disliked him. Just one step beyond dislike was hate.

Could Zora *hate* him?

She'd *dumped* him! Shouldn't he be the disliker in the relationship?

"Were your ears burning?" Felicia led Zora into the office. "We were just talking about you."

"Ummm." She looked as if she were about to have a heart attack. She was pale, and he could see the pulse jumping in her throat. Her heart was racing as fast as his, and that was way too fast.

"I'll go get Liam; he's upstairs with Timbo." Felicia flashed Zora a dazzling smile, the one that could get Liam to do absolutely anything. "Zora, have a seat there, in the chair next to Jake."

She smelled like a combination of flowers and something richer. For one stupid second, Jake wanted to lean over and just inhale her. But she wouldn't like that.

She wore a black T-shirt and soft-looking blue jeans. Her feet were in dark blue flip-flops, and her toes were a matching blue. He liked that—the thought she'd given to making her toenails the same color as her shoes. Or did she just like dark blue? He didn't know one damn thing about her. Not anymore.

What was he supposed to say to her? Jake had never felt tongue-tied around a woman, perhaps ever, definitely not since he was a teenager...and had been in love with her. *This* was that same feeling, the one he'd had right before he'd asked her to go with him to a movie.

And the feeling still sucked.

*Say something.*

"So. How about them—"

At the same time, she said, "Foggy, huh?"

They both broke off.

She folded her hands in her lap and looked down at them. "I have no idea what I'm doing here."

"Well, join the club. I never have a clue what I'm doing anywhere."

She smiled at that, and it was like sunlight breaking across her face, even though she was still looking at her lap. When was the last time she'd smiled at him, right into his eyes? A long, long time had passed since then.

Liam and Felicia came into the office, thank God. In the few seconds between their last words, Jake had forgotten the entire English language.

"Hey, there!" said Liam, reaching down to hug Zora.

Of course. People hugged. Jake had forgotten that. Should he have hugged her when she'd first walked in? That would have been nice. But no, if he'd done that, he'd have done something even more stupid than telling her he never knew what he was doing in the company offices. Gah. And besides, she didn't like him. He shouldn't press anything on her. He *had* hugged her out in the world, of course, when everyone else in the group was hugging. This was California, after all. It was practically the law. Had she hated it?

Had she been hating him this whole time?

Liam sat behind his desk. He grinned at Zora. "Forgive me if I'm jumping right to the point, but did you make up your mind?"

"Yes." Zora's voice was firm. "And it's yes."

The elation Jake felt at the simple word surprised him, as if the sun had just come up over the hill on a fresh, windy day. Maybe she didn't hate him, after all. Felicia was wrong. They'd just been running in parallel circles for years in town, but now their friends would overlap, and they'd have time to spend together. They could catch up. Put all the lost years behind them and just have a good time. For one second, Jake imagined having the kind of good time with her that he'd had once before. He was surprised to find he lost his breath a little. He coughed. "That's great. So great."

Felicia, sitting in a swivel chair next to Zora, smoothly handed her a file. In it, Jake knew, was the show's contract, the one he'd signed yesterday. "I have to admit, I'm surprised, but I'm thrilled. Our other contenders, of course, are exemplary women, but I couldn't get Jake interested in a single one of them. I think this is meant to be."

Zora sat straighter, her hands clasped in her lap. "Before we go any further, I do have one requirement."

"Anything," said Felicia, "within reason, of course."

"I don't want to date Jake. Can I date someone else while the show is being filmed? Maybe somebody from the crew?"

Jake sucked in a breath. He felt the tips of his ears go hot. So Felicia was right. She did hate him, after all. What the hell had he done? It couldn't have been about the breakup — that was too long ago. Had he done something personal to one of her close friends? This was Darling Bay, though. When he'd told Humphrey once that Molly Darling's orange muffin was stale that day — and that day only — he'd heard about Molly's displeasure from four different people. If he'd done something to offend Zora recently, he would've heard about it.

Apparently, she just hated him.

It didn't sit well. Jake might be a love-them-and-leave-them kind of guy like his brothers said he was, but his exes usually stuck around as friends. (Or they moved into the slip next to his.)

Felicia said with admirable restraint, "You do know that the other two Ballards are taken, don't you?" *One of them is mine.* She didn't say the words, but they hung in the air anyway.

"Reality TV is inherently fake, isn't it?" Zora looked at Felicia. "You always tell me that. That most of the stuff on television that we see is, if not scripted, heavily planned. Can't you plan for you and Liam to have a little fake fight?"

Felicia blinked. "We live together. We're just about as committed as can be. I don't think anyone would buy that. I don't think we'd fight and then he'd immediately go try to find a new girlfriend on national TV."

Zora turned to Liam. "Couldn't you try?"

Liam, who had that heated look in his eye that proceeded a rapid-fire angry barrel of words, said, "I don't want to date anyone who isn't Felicia. End of story. Not interested."

Nonplussed, Zora said, "Aidan then."

Liam shook his head. "And wreck the thing he's got going with Tuesday? He won't go for that. And isn't Tuesday a friend of yours from school? And what's the big deal, anyway?"

Felicia said "Yeah, you and Jake used to date. So what's the problem here?"

"That *is* the problem." Zora uncrossed and re-crossed her legs into exactly the same position. "We have a past, and why would we want to bring that back up? That's not interesting to viewers, right? What could be more boring? What about one of the handymen?"

"No." Felicia's voice was firm.

Jake caught a breath—apparently, he'd forgotten to breathe regularly ever since she stepped foot in the room. "Would it be that bad?"

Zora shot him a look of anger. Anger!

"Look," he started. "Whatever it is that's left-over between us—"

But Felicia interrupted him. Her voice was brusque. "Zora, it's Jake or no one. He *is* the show now. It's the Ballard Brothers, not the Ballards and their hired help. He's the reason twenty-five million people tuned in to the last season—they love Jake. They want to see him go on dates with pretty women. I'd prefer it be you—I think it'll make for good TV. But if it's not you, I'm fine with it being someone else, and I need to cast her, stat. I need to know right now if you're in or out."

Jake held his breath again. Pretty soon he was going to pass out from lack of oxygen. The elation that had filled him when she'd said yes was gone. She'd said yes to the show, not to him. She'd said yes to anyone *but* him.

Zora bit her bottom lip. Then she said, "I'm in."

And that clinched it for him. "Well, then, I'm out."

## NINE

Zora felt as if he'd slapped her. "Pardon?" Why couldn't she be a person who instinctively exclaimed, *What is your problem?* But she wasn't that person. Pardon was all she had.

Felicia apparently had no problem with stronger language. "Yeah, what the fuck, Jake?"

Jake shook his head and leaned forward, resting his elbows on his knees. He kept his head up, but he didn't look at Zora, only at Liam and Felicia. "She hates me. I'm not going to make a woman go on a show and *date* me if she hates me. I'm not a monster."

Felicia banged her pencil onto the desk. "She doesn't hate you! She's here to do the show."

"And she can. Use Bass, from the crew. Viewers love him."

"He's not a Ballard Brother."

Jake turned to Zora. "Do you?"

Zora felt like she'd been turned upside-down and shaken. "Do I what?"

"Hate me?"

"Of course not." Did she mean it? She couldn't actually tell. No, she didn't hate Jake. She had no feelings for him. No, strike that. She had immense feelings, apparently, about being turned down by him. That hurt. She should have seen it coming, and she hadn't. Would she never learn that Jake was bad for her?

Jake leaned forward. "But you avoid me."

"No, I don't."

"I never noticed it before today. But you do. When was the last time we had a polite conversation?"

"Yesterday."

"Before that, though? I talk to half the town every week, and that's before the weekend. But you and I haven't really talked since..."

Since they'd broken up.

Zora had made sure of that. If it had taken not going to more than half the parties she was invited to, she'd avoided him. And she did *not* want to talk about it.

She crossed her legs. "And I guess that's not going to change, since you're opting out of the show."

Felicia groaned. "He *cannot* opt out."

Jake tugged at his dark T-shirt. "I can, and I am. I'm not forcing her to work with me."

Wordlessly, Felicia held up a packet of paper. She shook it.

"I know," said Jake. "I signed it. But I'm canceling."

Liam, who'd been silent till now, said, "I don't think you want to do that. There's a penalty for cancelation, on either side."

Zora's stomach twisted.

Jake said, "I don't care. I'm not a monster. I'll pay it."

"It's fifty thousand."

His jaw dropped. "*Dollars?*"

What would have been an acceptable number to him? Twenty thousand? Twenty-five? How could she get *out* of here?

Felicia nodded. "In full. Before you ask, there's no payment plan. Don't forget I know you need the bonus for your big sailing trip."

If he considered it, that meant he'd be willing to pay fifty grand for the privilege of not doing the show with her. Was she *that* terrible?

Jake sputtered. "You mean the trip I'm never

going to be able to afford? Can't we just forget about the cancelation fee? In the spirit of family? Doesn't that buy me some rights to be an asshole when I need to?"

At least he'd noticed what he was being. That was a very small something. *Very* small, though.

"Nothing buys you those rights except fifty thousand dollars," said Felicia.

"Good God," said Zora, finally finding her feet in the conversation. "We can be adults about this, can't we? Let's just do the show. How hard can it be?"

Jake looked at her, his blue eyes saying something to her that she didn't want to understand. "Can I try something?"

"Um..."

"Shake my hand?"

Confused, she held out her hand. When he took it, a zap of static electricity snapped between them. She pulled her arm back. "Ow."

Jake kept his mouth shut, but Zora could read what he was thinking. *She can't even shake hands with me.*

"Look," she said. "I'm fine. You misread it. We're adults, right? Money is money." Zora had never been about money. She was a teacher, for God's sake. Now she was going to sell her soul for a television show?

No, not for a show. And not for him.

For a house of her own. That had to be worth it, right?

Jake shoved a hand through his hair. "But—"

Zora's throat was tight. "How hard can it be? You know how to build a house from scratch. That has to be harder than hanging out for a few weeks in the same location?"

Jake looked at her, his gaze pinned to hers. For a moment, it was as if they were alone. Liam and Felicia didn't exist. It was just the two of them, caught there in that moment, the only people in the world. A sensory memory smacked her so sharply she wondered if he could read it on her face. The memory of the way he used to hold her face in both hands, keeping himself inches from her lips until she would almost whimper for the kiss he always gave her. Eventually.

She took a shuddery breath and held it for a second before letting it go. She held his gaze, not wanting to lose what had become a staring contest that was turning her on in an embarrassing way.

Finally, he said, "Okay. You're right. How hard can it be?"

# TEN

How hard could it be? A week later, Zora admitted to herself it could be *hard*.

So much more difficult than she'd thought.

There had been paperwork, way more than she'd thought there would be. They'd run a background check, which didn't bother her since she'd passed one to work at the school, and a lie detector test, which *did* bother her. According to the polygraph examiner, she showed nervousness when it came to her truthfulness about past relationships. No, she'd never ghosted anyone. Why did the machine say she had? The only one she'd come close to ghosting was Jake, but she hadn't done that—she'd told him she was breaking up with him. That wasn't ghosting.

That day—so long ago now—had been brutal. She would have *preferred* to disappear on him without a trace, but it was Darling Bay, after all. Even though she was just eighteen, she knew that the town was small enough that she wouldn't be able to avoid him forever. She probably wouldn't even be able to avoid him for a week.

They'd met at their rock, the one on the beach at the west end of Hillmont. The rock they'd been perched on the first time he'd ever kissed her. Zora hadn't seen him in almost two weeks. It was her first trip out of the house since getting out of the hospital. Her mother had barely allowed her to go. "If he hurts you again, I'll kill him."

They were the strongest words Zora had ever heard her mother say. Usually Camille was worried about the world killing them in some insane way, not them killing anyone else.

Zora had beaten him there. The clouds were low, and the ocean was a dull roar in her ears that echoed her leaden feelings. She was in *love* with him, her blood was full of *Jake Jake Jake Jake*. His football letter jacket was heavy and warm, almost as good as having his arms around her.

But she couldn't be with him. Her mother was right. Being in a relationship was too dangerous. They'd proven *that*, hadn't they?

She saw him at the top of the cliff, peering over

like a miner looking down into a hole. She waved. He grinned in his full-body way, and instead of taking the winding path down, the one that most people used, he grabbed the rope affixed to a spike in the cliff and rappelled down, bouncing against the front of the cliff.

He ran to her, and before she could hold up her hands or tell him to calm down, that she had something she needed to say, he'd scooped her into his arms. He just said, "God, I missed you," and then he was kissing her like she was food or air—like she was something he needed in order to live.

And she felt the same way. He tasted like mint gum and life, like coffee and love. His tongue, sure and sweet, aroused her instantly, and she felt him get hard against her. She needed him—she couldn't do this, couldn't break both their hearts—

But she needed to let him go. Zora was old enough to know she wasn't grown up yet even though she *felt* she was. He was going to grow up, too, and need things, the way people did. And she wouldn't be able to give him what he needed.

So she pulled back. She placed a few inches of ocean air between them, instantly feeling chilled to the bone.

"Hi." He tugged at a lock of her hair. "I missed you so much. Two whole weeks without you! I felt like I was dying."

*He'd* felt like that?

It only deepened her resolve. She'd spent hours rehearsing what she'd say. *I love you so much, but we're not right for each other. I have to let you go so that we can both grow in the way we need to. It's better this way. In the long run, we'll both know this.*

Instead, what came out was, "We're over."

He laughed. He *laughed!* "Don't scare me like that."

His plaid flannel was open, and she wanted to press herself against his soft blue T-shirt so badly it almost hurt. "I mean it. We're done."

It was astonishing, the way his face closed so quickly. She'd never seen his expression quite like this—Jake Ballard was the class clown, the cutup, the guy who made everyone laugh, even the teachers.

But apparently, he also knew how to retreat.

Because he was gone already.

He stuck his hands under his armpits, his eyes narrow. "Oh, yeah? Why?"

"Because I say so." It was so unlike her, this answer, but it was the only one she had that was true, and she just didn't think she could lie to him.

The heartbreaker of it was that he didn't.

"Are you going to change your mind?" His gaze was tied to hers—she couldn't have torn hers away if she'd tried.

So she didn't try. She let herself get lost in those deep blue eyes—deeper than the ocean they stood on the edge of—for the very last time. Finally, after two long, painful breaths, she said, "I'm not." She slipped off the letter jacket and held it out. He took it from her and stuck it under his arm.

He didn't say goodbye. He didn't say anything at all.

He just nodded once and closed his eyes. When he opened them again, he was already gone.

If anyone had ghosted that relationship, it was her. Maybe that was why the lie detector showed nervousness around those questions.

Now, all these years later, she was going into a business agreement with him. Insane.

*A house is not insane. This is the best way forward.*

Today was the first day of actual filming, and Zora wondered if they'd edit it out if she vomited into a trash can out of nervousness. They'd probably leave it in for pizzazz, she figured, so she'd just eaten a piece of dry toast for breakfast.

This was it. She'd probably have to look at him today. She had talked more to Jake in the last week of prep than she had since they'd broken up. Something was still there, she had to admit it—a chemistry she couldn't just shut down. There was that shock thing, the way electricity snapped between them whenever they got too close, which she wasn't willing to do much more of. His dark blue gaze still held that oceans-deep look, the one that could make her feel like drowning.

She would just keep her eyeballs off his face and lie to herself that it wasn't the most difficult thing she'd ever done.

"Ow," said Zora.

Tony, one of the camera people, was clipping her mic pack to her back. So far, he'd pinched her skin and pulled her hair. He didn't say sorry, either —he was busy chattering to the woman fussing with the iPad, Anna. "And I just said if Angelina wasn't going to be at the opening, then neither would I!"

Anna laughed. "You're so full of it."

They were in the metal shop of Ballard Brothers Construction, which looked like it had been cleared out to store audio-video equipment. She and Jake were supposed to be getting ready for filming the first house, but he hadn't shown his face yet.

Maybe he'd forgotten it was today.

Or maybe he'd changed his mind. Perhaps she still had a hope of getting out of this.

No, he'd show, and this was going to be terrible. She wished that she'd been able to do the show with anyone else. Even careless Tony with his pinching and pulling.

Tony said to Anna, "I know. But I swear, I *did* see her at the mall with one of her forty-two children just last week."

"Yeah, I'm guessing she doesn't shop in Burbank."

"Stars," said Tony. Together, he and Anna said, "They're just like us."

Zora desperately wanted to lick her lips, which were heavy with lip stain and thick gloss, but the makeup woman had warned her not to. The foundation was thick on her face, and her eyelashes felt heavy with mascara. She almost hadn't recognized herself in the mirror when the woman had finished. She reminded herself of the group of women who ran the Darling Bay Rose Society auction, all false color and high cheekbones and smoky eyes that looked expensive. Zora hated it. But it was somehow part of this whole TV deal, so...

She tugged at the cord now trailing under her armpit. Would her sweat short it out? Could she get electrocuted this way? "Do I really need this? Can't I just project my voice? I'm a teacher and—"

Tony clucked his tongue at her. "Shhh, sweetie. It's fine." He did something with a piece of metal that looked like a bobby pin and declared her done. "Now all you need to do is get into hair and makeup."

Zora's cheeks burned. She looked at her shoes, a

low wedge that she was deathly afraid that she would trip in. The heel wasn't high, but it was higher than her Converse. "I already did that."

"Tony!" Anna looked as horrified as Zora felt.

He pulled his ball cap lower on his head. "Whoops." And he was gone, waving a clipboard at someone Zora hadn't been introduced to yet.

Anna said, "He's an idiot. Ignore him."

"Do I look that bad?" Zora asked.

Anna folded her lips and shook her head. Awesome. Way to inspire confidence.

"Turn around, let me see?"

Jake's voice. Yeah, because *that* was what she needed, Jake telling her that she looked terrible. She already knew that from Tony's response—she didn't need his help.

"That's okay," she said, deliberately moving forward so she wouldn't have to turn around. The problem was that the only thing in front of her was a few feet of workbench and a small dorm-sized fridge. Maybe she needed a soda—she *definitely* needed to catch her breath before she turned to face him. She reached out and pulled open the fridge door.

"No—you shouldn't do that—"

A stench like no other hit her smack dab in the face. It was a terrible combination of fish guts and excrement and maybe something a little sweet, like rotten bananas. It was a punch of disgustingness. She smacked the door shut and covered her mouth. Through a cough, she managed, "What *is* that? And why are you *keeping* it?"

"It's a little experiment of mine."

"Are you dabbling in chemical warfare?"

"It's for fishing."

Zora pulled her arm out of her sweatshirt and held the fabric up to her nose, grateful to have a reason to cover the lower half of her painted face. "Are you fishing for *Satan?* Because I think that's what you pulled up, honestly."

"Yeah, I think it backfired. I thought maybe if I used durian as bait then it'd smell so strong that fish wouldn't be able to resist it."

"Durian, like that fruit that tastes good but smells bad?"

He nodded, his blue eyes sparkling. It shouldn't be legal from him to look that delightful this early in the morning. With his rumpled dark hair, gray T-shirt, and long red board shorts, he looked like he'd just walked out of the pages of a boating catalog.

And she, apparently, looked awful, despite the way they'd glammed her up.

Jake said, "They say it's the worst smell in the world."

She kept the sweatshirt up high, almost covering her eyes. "Did it work?"

He shook his head. "Not so far. I haven't figured out a way to carry it to the marina with me. I don't want to put it in my car."

"You know that the fridge is unusable now, right?" She felt schoolmarmish pointing it out. "For the next three thousand years."

The corner of his mouth pulled up. "Yeah. But it's useful sometimes. I put a T-shirt of Liam's in there for an hour last week, and then put it back in his closet."

Behind the fabric, Zora snorted. That was pretty good. The mic cord tugged again at her hair. Were they already recording? Should she be careful of her modulation, of how her words were enunciated? Or did that come later? "How did that go?"

Jake wrinkled his perfect nose at her. "So *good*. He doesn't have the best sense of smell, so he put it on and somehow thought it was a skunk passing by outside. By the time he'd walked to the cafe, the smell had gotten unnoticeable to him, I guess. He cleared the place out. Someone called in a gas leak, and by the time the smell got traced to him, the whole cafe was out on the sidewalk."

She had to give it to him, that was pretty funny. "What did Felicia say about it?"

From behind them came Felicia's voice. "Felicia told him to get everything in that closet dry-cleaned, and she thanked her lucky stars that she'd insisted on her own closet. And I wouldn't let him come to bed that night till he'd taken three showers. You're an awful brother, Jake."

He grinned at the showrunner. "You worship me."

"Who doesn't?" Felicia winked at Zora. "Come on, Zora, let's get out of the smell so you can unmask yourself."

"When do we start?" Tentatively, she let the sweatshirt drop from in front of her face.

"Right now." Felicia hit the garage door opener on the wall and gestured to the driveway. "Both of you, hop in my car, and we'll go to the first place. Camera crew will be right behind us. Jake, honey, did you do hair and makeup?"

He flopped bank the hank of brown hair that had fallen over his forehead. "I don't need it."

"Your choice."

His choice? Zora said, "Hey, wait, I didn't *have* to look like a hooker?" She paused. "No, scratch that. Prostitutes deserve respect. I didn't have to look like a clown at the circus?"

Felicia said, "Darling, that smoky eye is delicious."

Zora tilted her head. "Sexist! Why doesn't *he* have to have a smoky eye?" Then, for a brief and startling second, she imagined Jake wearing guyliner, his eyes smoldering even more than they normally were.

It wouldn't be safe to have a man like him wear a smoky eye. Women would crash their cars if he so much as glanced at them.

Felicia said, "Well, it helps your features stand out on camera. It's just what we do."

Zora didn't want to make waves—she really didn't. She wanted to get this over with, to get it done so that she could get home and back to the romance novel that was at this very moment resting on the pillow next to hers. "But...do I *have* to wear it?"

Jake said, "Yeah, does she?"

Oh, God, did she look so bad that he thought she needed his help?

He stopped in his tracks and crossed his arms. "Because she looks prettier without it."

Now, that was a straight-up lie. She looked as if she were wearing an Instagram filter. All she was missing was black fuzzy cat ears. *Or* was he saying that she looked like crap now? "Don't need rescuing, Jake"

"I'm not—"

"No, you don't have to wear it." Felicia looked impatient as she stood midstride halfway between them and her car. "But you do look great. You'll play great on camera."

Zora paused.

"Do whatever you want to do," said Jake softly. "*We* run this show now."

Or she could be herself.

Which meant pale, washed out, no lips, limp hair. What would her mother say? (Camille would be horrified if it were someone else. She'd talk trash with Evelyn in 119 about why the girl on the TV couldn't at least wear a little blush.)

The important thing wasn't how she looked. After all, she was never going to watch the show.

The important thing was buying a house and being able, someday, to call it home.

"It's okay, I'll keep it on. Maybe they can go a little lighter next time."

Felicia had already nodded and was striding ahead, starting at her cell phone. "Mmm, great."

Zora ground her teeth together and followed.

## ELEVEN

The inside of Felicia's car smelled delicious, Jake thought. It smelled like expensive perfume and leather—the show always provided Felicia with a new lease every year— but what *really* smelled good was that hint of lemon hanging in the air.

He'd forgotten that completely. How could he have? Zora had always smelled lightly of lemons and sugar, as if she were made of lemonade, even back in high school. It was the smell of sunshine—clean and crisp, like laundry dried on the line. He'd taken the backseat, so he leaned forward. "Hey, Zora, do you have a dryer?"

She turned slightly so that he could see the pink makeup piled on her cheeks. She was so right—she didn't need that stuff. "Huh?"

"Or do you line-dry your clothes?"

Felicia gave a light laugh. "Don't mind him, he's always trying to get us to dry our clothes outside. He's obsessed."

Zora narrowed her eyes. "How did you know?"

Satisfied, he sank back into his seat. "Knew it. You smell like it."

"I smell?"

"Like line-dried clothing. It's the best smell, right?"

Zora's eyes were wide. "Mmm."

God, she seemed tense. Jake was doing his best to ignore her tension, but it was thick in the air, feeling like the opposite of her lemony scent. "You don't need to be nervous. We just have to be ourselves, and that's easy."

She said, "Where *is* the house?"

Jake peered out the window. "Almost there."

"And you're really not going to tell me what house it is before we get there."

"Where would the fun in that be?"

Felicia parked about a block away. They were being recorded in Felicia's car, but Jake knew enough now about how it all worked that it would be better to get her full facial reaction with the whole crew there when she saw the house.

Because she was going to die.

Jake wasn't a betting man, but if he were, he'd

lay money that this first one would be the house she chose out of the three they planned to show her. It had everything, an ocean view, a hot tub, three bedrooms, which would be great for an office and a guest room (or a nursery? He didn't know her life, after all, not anymore. And while he knew a lot of gossip about a lot of the town, he realized that he kind of avoided hearing any about her. Huh).

Felicia was already out of the car, striding down the block, her cell phone at her ear.

"Come on," he said, shooting Zora a smile. "Let's do this."

She flipped down the visor and looked in the mirror. He could see from the side that she grimaced. She glanced back and said, "Do I really look as terrible as I think I do?"

He paused and could instantly see he'd made a mistake by doing so.

She sighed. "Never mind."

"No! You look gorgeous. It's just that you don't need all that stuff."

Zora blew out an audible breath and held up a hand. "Whatever you say will just make it worse, so I suggest you don't say anything at all. I think the same thing. Let's do this." She plastered on a smile, and while Jake could see it was an effort, he couldn't help feeling buoyed. Maybe this would be okay.

And maybe he could get over himself and his own worries for a minute and just try to have fun. What else was the point?

They spent a moment waiting at the end of the block while the camera crew made sure they had the right sound and light levels. The street ended in a T. If they went left, the houses down the hill were smaller and more inexpensive. If they went right, the housing got fancier the wider the view of the ocean they had. Ridiculous, really. If you wanted a view of the ocean, you should live on a boat. Jake had the best view of all, and his slip cost just three hundred a month.

But they'd parked there on purpose. They all knew Felicia would expect them to head down the hill, to the cheaper houses. This was going to be great.

"Everything ready?" Felicia's voice was authoritative.

Anna and Tony nodded, looking at their equipment. Another camera guy had joined them—Jake thought his name was Fred but wasn't quite sure.

Zora also nodded, gazing downhill.

"Let's go," Jake said. Tony swung his camera toward Zora.

Sure enough, the look on her face when they started walking uphill was priceless. Jake was no expert on TV since the only one he watched was in the Golden Spike, but he could tell her expression would play well later.

"Wait," she said. She took a few rapid steps to catch up to them. "I can't afford up. Just down. And that's only a maybe."

Felicia looked over her shoulder, her mouth pressed in a friendly but firm line. She didn't say anything.

Jake was in charge now that the cameras were rolling. "Liam ran the numbers. He knows what you can afford."

"But I bet realtors don't listen to that, right? Isn't it their job to sell you too much house?"

He wished he could say something like, *With the down payment they're giving you, you can afford a LOT more house*, but part of the contract said they couldn't talk about payment while on screen. "Not my brother. Not this show. You can afford this."

Zora gave him a strained smile as she bit her lower lip, and suddenly, he was struck by the urge to do the same to her. To catch her in his arms and nibble on the same lip. To see what it tasted like under all that lipstick. To make her laugh when his own lips came away fire-engine red.

It was such a visceral urge he had to still his left hand from reaching to catch hers.

Weird.

He'd been a teenager when they'd dated, a kid. He was over her.

"There must be some kind of shack up here that I don't remember, because I don't think that..." Her voice trailed off as she saw it, and Jake made sure the camera was back on her. "Oh...Oh, *no* way."

Which would have been great except she sounded like she actually meant it.

# TWELVE

"No. Uh-uh. That house is not for me." Zora hated everything about it. "But thank you." She should probably be polite about it, when in fact she just wanted to run screaming down the hill, past Felicia's car, all the way into downtown Darling Bay. She could be inside her own beloved rented cottage in six minutes, five if she stopped screaming and saved her breath.

Jake was looking at her like she was crazy.

Fair enough—that was how she felt. Probably anyone else in the whole world would have been excited if this was a house they were being offered. She was the anomaly, the one in a million.

The house was phenomenal, she gave it that. It wasn't huge, but it commanded an awe-inspiring view of the marina down below. It was modern, glass and steel glinting in the sun.

She and Jake made their way indoors, the crew ahead and behind them, catching every ridiculous expression on her face.

And inside, it was more of the same. Modern, clean, elegant.

Everything she was not.

It was spectacular, the way the sea danced into the rooms, the way it felt like being in a jewel box. Sunset Magazine could have done a spread on it.

She hated it.

Finally, she tuned back in to what Jake was saying. "It only has two bedrooms, and I know Liam was hoping for three so that you could have an office *and* a guest room. But it fits in your budget because it's small for this side of the hill. It's turnkey—you could move in tomorrow."

Desperately, Zora said, "I thought the show was about doing construction and renovation. What would Aiden do here?"

"You'd just have to find something for him to do. Maybe you need an in-law unit in the backyard, someplace you could rent out to visiting artists. Or maybe you want more skylights." He looked up at the soaring beams and spread his hands wide as if he were ready to present the house to her right now.

"Use your imagination. What would make this house a home for you?"

"Nothing," she gasped. "This is not my house. Get me out." She charged for the door.

Pulling the whole crew and making the walk back down to their waiting cars was not just painful—it was completely humiliating. Sweat poured down Zora's back, and she wasn't even hot. It was the sweat of regret. She should never have agreed to this—she was going to look like a fool in front of the whole nation. She didn't consider herself that proud, but boy, this was going to be a blow to her ego.

Jake caught up to her. "Okay, timeout. Timeout."

She glanced behind her and noticed that at least one camera was trained on her, so it wasn't a timeout in the off-the-record way. "I'm sorry, I really am. I'm being horribly ungrateful." A cold, sick shiver broke her skin into goosebumps. "I honestly thought I wouldn't care about how I'm seen on TV, but knowing that I'm going to look like the most over-privileged princess who doesn't want a gorgeous house with a million-dollar view—okay..." She leaned forward and put her hands on her thighs. "Yeah, that makes me want to die." She looked up at him. "Can I die? Is that in the contract? If I kick the bucket, will they at least pull the show?"

He squatted so that he was on her level. "I think if you die, then the ratings will skyrocket. It'll make even more people watch you bolt from that house that most would literally stab their own mothers to live in."

"I like my mother. No stabbing."

"Okay, that's fine. No dying either, though, okay?"

Zora slowly straightened. "I'm terrible at this."

His lips went sideways in a wry nod. "You're not very good at it, that's true."

"Is it going to be this bad at the next house?"

He shrugged. "It's the opposite of this one, so maybe not."

"Oh, boy." When she looked up at him, his eyes were soft. She'd forgotten this, that he could always soothe her.

She tried to ignore the fact that, just for one second, she desperately wanted to lean into him. She wanted to press herself against his chest and feel his lips against her temple. It was ridiculous and juvenile, but she wanted him to wrap his arms around her as he had when she was eighteen and she thought he could protect her from everything.

When she'd wanted him to.

THE NEXT HOUSE *was* the opposite, and not in a good way.

At least when Zora stepped foot in the 1970s ranch house, she didn't want to rip her own skin off. It wasn't a modern gem, it was just a house. A *huge* house. It was three-thousand square feet, about two thousand more than she needed. It had five bedrooms plus two living rooms and a bonus room.

As she wandered through them all, she tried *so* hard to imagine herself living inside these walls. Could she put Mr. Prickles's cat tree there? Could she make that corner into a reading nook?

But she just couldn't imagine it.

This was a house for a family. A nice, suburban family whose biggest fights revolved around who last walked the dog and where the Yahtzee game was. This wasn't a house for a single teacher who went to other people's houses for dinner.

The place was big and pretty and average. There wasn't a quirk in the whole place. Not one. Even the tiki bar in the backyard looked like it had come from a Costco kit.

Jake showed her (again), how silently the closet opened in the fourth bedroom, just like he had in the previous three. "Can you hear that? I can't hear that."

"Why should opening a closet be a secret?"

He laughed. "I have no idea. Liam's the realtor —I just know he's always happy with quiet doors. That's a good question."

"I don't even have enough clothes to fill one of these closets."

"You'll have to buy more clothes."

He was still a sweetie, she had to admit. He was looking at her like she was funny, as if she were interesting. She wasn't *not* those things, but honestly, she knew this was going to be a dry episode. Hopefully the cameras were more focused on him than they were her.

Jake led her out of the bedroom and through the bonus room. "Have you taken a good look at the wet bar?"

"What's the difference between a dry and a wet bar?" Oh, why had she asked? She didn't *care*.

But Jake looked so pleased to be able to answer. "It has a sink!"

"Who has a wet bar in their house, anyway? Alcoholics, that's who."

"Or people who like to have a good time."

"With alcohol."

"And running water." Jake looked over his shoulder. Zora saw Anna give them a keep-rolling sign with her finger.

Keep rolling? There was nothing to roll about.

This place felt so generic. She wanted out. Not as desperately as she had the glass nightmare, but there was no point in being here anymore.

"I'm not feeling this one, I hate to say it."

Jake glanced down at his clipboard as if he could pull out more information that might change her mind. "It's connected to sewer, you know. No septic over here."

"Major selling point. Yep. Who doesn't love thinking about where their poop will go?" That wasn't fair. Knowing where your poop went was surely a very important part of buying a house. It should have been fascinating to her. She should have wanted to know the type of pipe that would shoot her poop away from the house.

The problem was none of this felt real. It was as if she was in a dream, a really long and kind of boring dream. She drove her nails into her palm and it hurt. Then she couldn't remember, did things hurt in dreams or not?

"This is going to be a wonderful house for the right family. But I have to feel something. Some kind of jolt. You know?"

"I do," said Jake. He came close enough to give her a small, quiet high-five. In between their hands, that predictable spark jumped.

THE THIRD AND last house was so pretty! Zora felt her heart lighten at the sight of it. It was a small yellow bungalow with a bright red door, shutters that looked real and usable, and a postage-stamp garden full of roses.

Jake, leading her through the garden and up the porch, pushed open the door with ceremony. "Built in 1927, this is probably the most picturesque, and I don't mean that in realty terms, like Liam would. I just think it's pretty as a picture." He gave her a look when he said the last part, and something in his voice made Zora's cheeks flush.

Then she wondered if the face powder was holding or if she was greasy as a griddle.

The door opened into a yellow living room. To the left, there was a fireplace with a carved wooden mantle. Bookcases lined the right wall. It smelled good, like cedar and sunshine.

"Isn't this pretty?"

Zora agreed. "Pretty. Yes." It was just perfect.

But there was no spark. This was a house she'd visit and enjoy. She peeked into the bathroom and the two small bedrooms. More of the same. The rooms were both charming and appealing.

It was meant to be lived in by a young couple who wanted—and then had—a baby. They'd coo at the child at the built-in dining room nook. He'd learn to run in socks on the hardwood floors. They'd move when the second one got too big and they wanted a room for each child.

"Why is it on the market?"

Jake smiled. "Young family, two kids. Wanted a bit more room."

Zora swallowed.

Jake kept up a running monologue, but after another turn around the house, she realized she hadn't been listening to him—she'd just been watching the way his mouth moved. Suddenly—viscerally—she remembered exactly how it had felt to kiss him. God, she'd been so young, such a long time ago now, but it all flooded back to her—the way his mouth could catch hers and take it, his lips strong and sure. Her heart dipped, dropping almost all the way into her stomach. He was still as good-looking as he'd been then, only more so now. His jaw was wider, his neck thicker. He wasn't a boy anymore. Jake was all man, and she didn't let herself speculate on how else he'd changed.

She didn't want this house. It wasn't right. Desperation thrummed inside her lungs. "I don't want it."

Jake looked justifiably confused. "No horizontal blinds? We can do vertical. Or bottom-up?"

"No. No nothing. Not here. This isn't the house for me."

"Okay, then." He moved forward, a slow smile

spreading, his hands outstretched as if he were trying to quiet a spooked horse. "Easy, now. No big deal. One of the other two, then. We can find a way to make it work."

Zora was *not* a horse to be whispered. "No. I hate all three. None of them are me, even if you fix them up. I can't picture myself in any of them." Politeness got the better of her, again. "I'm sorry. I can't believe I'm wasting your time like this. This isn't fair to anyone. But—"

"I know," he said calmly. "Lots of people feel like this..."

She tuned him out as her cell phone rang. She'd been warned, of course, to keep it turned off so she wouldn't ruin a shoot. And she *had* put it on silent, so she knew it was her mother, the only person who could ring through at any time. "Jake, I'm sorry."

He shrugged amiably. "You do you."

Tony, the cameraman, shot her a dirty look, but what was the big deal? It wasn't like they were scripted.

"Hi, Mom." She ducked left into a perfect little pantry. It was the size of a walk-in closet and smelled like vanilla. It also made her want to accidentally drop a bag of flour on the floor just so something would need to be cleaned up. "Is this an emergency? Because—"

"Honey, I'm at your house, and it's really not a

big deal, everything's okay now, but you might want to come over here. Can you come?"

"Wait, what?" Zora's mind spun. "And what?" Her mother had keys, yes, but she didn't usually go over without a good reason, and never without asking.

"I reckon you best hurry, too, sweetie—a fire-fighter said he knew your landlord—what's his name?"

"Denny?"

"Yeah, him. I think he was going to call him."

"What did you do?"

"I kind of tapped the front of your place."

"Tapped?"

"With my car."

# THIRTEEN

Jake drove—Zora didn't talk, her face drawn and tight. He didn't press her to speak, although he wanted to. She thrummed with tension that he could almost feel.

"Here," she finally said at a small house behind the school. She made a gasping noise, then she pushed out of his car and ran up the driveway.

Whatever her mother had done to the house, it hadn't been a tap like Zora had said. It was the kind of damage that would undoubtedly end up on the front page of the *Darling Bay Gazette*, and sure enough, Domenico Patton was already using his iPhone to click pictures from the street.

The rear end of a red economy car stuck out of the front of the small cottage. The car had run over a low white wooden gate, taking out an arbor on its way. Wheel marks rutted the dirt, and pieces of interior drywall were still dropping inside the jagged open edge of the house. Glass from the windows clinked under firefighter boots. Somehow it looked obscene, a house peeled open like a can of fruit cocktail. Three men were stomping around the car, using boards to prop up sections of the house. A smell of scorched paper and gasoline hung in the air.

Zora hadn't even stopped to gawk—she'd disappeared into the house through the open and surprisingly still-usable front door. Jake followed, jumping out of the way as a firefighter tossed a piece of broken wood his direction. Tox Ellis tried to stop him from entering what appeared to have been a living room, but he wasn't interested in looking at the wreckage.

"Where's Zora?" he asked the fire captain.

"With her mom and the ambulance in the backyard." Tox pointed with a meaty thumb to the side. "We're going to declare the whole building unstable until code compliance and the building department get out here, so I need you out."

Jake nodded and sped around the house. The garden in the rear was undamaged. Sun shone on rows of flowers, and he noticed a low rumble from a beehive on his left. It was idyllic, as if nothing had happened. His heart raced.

Zora was kneeling at her mother's feet. "Mom. You've got to remember *something*."

Camille Turner shook her head. There was a cut on her cheek trickling blood, but otherwise, she looked okay. Next to them, the ambulance crew was packing their bags. "I told you. It's all a blur."

"Tell me about the blur, then."

"No, more like a blank. There's just nothing there in my memory."

"Are you saying you have amnesia?"

Zora reached to wipe the blood, but her mother batted away her hands impatiently. "That's it. I have amnesia from right before the crash. I think it was the car, honestly. What if my car is one of those that the accelerator gets stuck? Didn't people die from that? I could have died. The car just took off without me in charge of it." She looked up. "Jake Ballard! What a pleasure to see a good-looking man around here!"

Two of the medics grumbled good-naturedly, but Camille ignored them. "Come sit here." She patted the seat next to her, and Jake sat.

"Hi, Mrs. Turner." Jake smiled. He'd always liked Zora's mother, though she'd obviously hated him after they broke up, almost spitting at him like an angry cat when they bumped into each other in town. Apparently she didn't hate him now.

"Did you hear I have amnesia? I'm a fascinating case. I could tell you stories. But I wouldn't remember the end of them! Ha!"

Zora leaned forward to stand from kneeling, giving Jake a brief glance into her shirt. He only caught sight of the top of her bra, pale pink, and the slight valley between her breasts. It felt wrong to see. But yeah, he sure as hell looked.

"If you have amnesia, Mom, you have to go to the hospital. No two ways about it."

"But—"

"Don't argue with me." Her voice was firm.

What would that be like? To have a relative old enough to make the transfer from the caretaker to the cared? Jake and his brothers had been raised by Bill Ballard, and he'd died early, just like their parents had. There was no one to watch slide into old age, no one to take clues from.

"I swear to you. I *did* have amnesia. It was like a black cloud filling my brain. I could barely remember my own name!"

Bonnie Maddern stopped repacking a red bag. "You want to go with us, Mrs. Turner? The offer still stands."

"I hate hospitals."

Zora said, "Amnesiacs stay in hospitals until

they regain their memories. Isn't that what they do on your soaps?"

Jake admired how soft and loving she kept her voice.

Camille folded her arms. "Well, I can feel it coming back to me now. Slowly."

"Good," said Zora. She sat on the other side of the bench. "Tell me how it happened."

Staring at her lap, Camille said in a low voice. "I just got a little confused, I guess."

"Like at the post office that one day?"

Camille nodded.

"We need to go see the doctor."

"He'll tell me I have to stop driving."

"Maybe that could be a good idea?" Zora's voice was soft, and she took her mother's hand.

A single tear ran down Camille's face. "Then I'll be old."

"You'll never be old, Mama."

Something warmed in Jake's core, exactly as if someone had lit a candle inside him. It was a kind of dizzy feeling, and it wasn't actually that comfortable. He'd just plain forgotten how sweet Zora could be. Sweet and melty, with that directness that used to shoot through him unexpectedly. He felt that zing right now, watching her hold her mother's hand.

"Are you mad at me?" Camille fretted with the

hem of her blouse.

"I don't know." Zora sighed.

"Don't be mad. Please don't be."

Zora pushed back a lock of Camille's hair. She didn't seem to be aware of the identical lock hanging in front of her own eyes. "Okay. I'm not angry. I'm just worried. Did anyone call Denny, do you know?"

Camille nodded, looking miserable. "One of the firefighters said he did."

Zora winced. "That's not going to be fun."

"Denny Sydenham owns this house?" Jake couldn't stand the guy. He was a pompous windbag who had married a Southern California elderly socialite who had then died, leaving him all her money. He'd bought up dozens of small houses, flipping them into Airbnbs and driving up rent all over town. If he'd been a nicer guy, Jake could have forgiven him the short-term rentals. Business was business, and the busier Darling Bay was, the better for everyone, overall. But the way he *acted*. Like he was King of the Town, when everyone knew that title actually went to Hawk Stokell who was in charge of playing Santa each year. Also, everyone liked Hawk because he was actually *likable*, the opposite of Denny.

"Yeah. And I know he wants to convert it into

another vacation rental. He *hates* that I put in the vegetable garden—he wanted to xeriscape."

The far garden gate slapped open as Denny himself stalked in. "Hell, yeah, I wanted zeroscopy or whatchacallit! Desert plants! Succulents! Not a drop of water! Not like this—"

Zora's hands were on her hips. "You *know* I use gray-water for this. I haul out buckets of laundry rinse, and I've never used a drop of fresh water. Besides, what do you care? I pay for water anyway."

Good for her. She was going to put up a fight for a thing that didn't really matter, probably in the hope that he'd blow out his bluster by the time he got to shouting about the car that had just plowed into his house.

But of course, it didn't work for long.

Denny pointed a knobby finger at Camille. "You! I've been telling you for *years* that you shouldn't be driving. You're a menace and a threat to life!"

Camille, who had been shaking and tremulous until now, straightened. "I drive better than you do, Denny Sydenham. I saw you driving home the other night, drunk as a skunk, weaving all over the road. Who do you think called the cops and got you arrested for drunk driving? I stayed on the line with Lexie until I saw them pull you over."

Denny bared his yellow teeth at her. "Didn't get

arrested, did I? Only weavin' because I was doing a Sudoku on my phone, and there's no way to prove *that*, is there? You *know* you're going to pay for rebuilding the whole front of my house, don't you?"

Camille tossed her long silver hair over her shoulder. "Fiddle-faddle. That's what your home insurance is for. You've got more money than God. Won't be any skin off your nose."

"Not my fault you're too old to drive, and hell no, I ain't gonna let my insurance rise. That'll be yours if I've got to drag you to court by your thumbs."

Nope, it didn't get to go ugly, especially with Zora's mom, and the cameras still filming in the background.

Jake stood and said, "I'm sure we can sort this all out later when everyone's had a chance to cool off and we know the extent of the damage. I can get Aidan to come out and give an estimate for repair, even if you end up using someone else. You want me to get that ball rolling? And in the meantime, maybe I can drive you over to the hospital just for a quick check. What do you think, Mrs. Turner?"

"If you make it brandy at the Golden Spike, yes, I'm in shape to make it that far."

Zora, the tops of her cheeks pink, said, "No, we stay here, Mom. Denny's right. It'll come out of your auto insurance."

Camille looked stricken. "But that'll make your premium soar, won't it?"

"My premium?" Zora shook her head. "No, your premium. It was your car."

Camille's eyes widened. "I thought you got me on your policy."

"Mom."

Camille bit her lip. "Oops."

"MOTHER. *Seriously?*"

FOURTEEN

Zora felt anger light her vision red, and at the same time, she felt sick to her stomach. It was all made so much worse by being in front of a camera crew. They wouldn't turn off their cameras, no matter how many times she dragged her finger over her throat. She lowered her voice as much as possible. "You have to be kidding, right?" But she knew Camille, who loved a practical joke, wouldn't take something this far.

"Oh, honey, I'm so sorry. I really thought you said that."

The only time they'd ever talked about car insurance was two years before when Zora had said she liked her policy and did her mother want the name of the agent. "I *didn't*."

"Well, bother." Camille slumped back onto the bench. "I suppose I'll have to buy some, so they can pay this off. I wonder how much that will cost."

Denny was almost hopping up and down now, and it wouldn't have surprised Zora to see puffs of white smoke steaming up from his sweaty bald head. "You don't have *insurance?* I *knew* I should have sold this place last year when the values were higher. I don't even want this place anymore! You've ruined the backyard with all these *flowers* and *vegetables*." For some reason, he put the words into air quotes. "And now my house has a car in the living room. Zora, consider this your thirty-days-notice. And Camille, I'm gonna take you to court for all you got, lady." He jabbed a finger in her mother's direction.

Zora moved so close in front of him that he had to drop his hand. "Don't you *dare* yell at my mother. This house has been falling down the whole time I've lived here. There's dry rot in the attic, the foundation is cracked, and termites have almost taken down the back porch. The reason I carry my laundry rinse water out and put it on the flowers is that the drains are perennially clogged by the roots you refuse to take care of. Every other month I pay out of my own pocket for Vinay to come out and unclog the kitchen sink because you make such a fuss when I ask you to get it done for me." Of course

—it occurred to her too late—the house was probably uninhabitable now, due to her mother, and all of this was moot. She managed, "You're a terrible landlord, and you can't evict me—I'm giving my notice! Come on, Mom."

She heard an actual whir as a camera zoomed in on her face—was she as red and sweaty as she felt? Probably.

"Where are we going?"

"You wanted a drink, right? I'm going to join you if you're still sure you don't want to get checked out." Her mother could make her own decisions—she certainly had with her lack of car insurance.

But Denny moved toward her surprisingly quickly. He stepped an inch too close. Zora flinched, and she couldn't help it—she took a step backward. She felt sudden fear, as if he were going to do something physical, something she couldn't stop.

His voice was guttural. "The only thing I care about is how you'll pay for this. If you even think you're going to—"

Then Jake was between them. "Nope."

Denny panted a wet, angry breath. "*What?*"

"Nope, you don't get to talk to her like that. You can leave now." His body was broad, and he completely blocked Zora's view of her steaming landlord.

For just one second, she let herself enjoy it. A man—this man, always the gold standard of sexiness as far as she was concerned, though she didn't think of him like that anymore —standing up for her in the old-fashioned sense of the word. Willing to fight her battles for her.

But that was the problem. No one fought her battles for her but Zora herself. That had been true for a really long time. And that was how she wanted it.

So she gently pushed Jake to the side. He moved after giving her a quizzical look.

"Thanks," she said, her heart thundering in her chest. "But I've got this. Denny, can we meet to-morrow to talk options? We're both overwrought right now."

"I am *not* overwrought!" He stomped his foot too close to her own.

"Let's meet up tomorrow."

"Did you even *see* what it looks like at the front of the house? It's a nightmare!"

"Let's talk tomorrow." She kept her voice even and calm, though she didn't feel it.

Denny shoved his hands into his jacket pockets. "*Fine.* But you'd better have your ducks in a row and be ready to tell me how you're going to fix all this."

"Oh, I surely will." She took the step forward

that she'd lost to him before, and this time it was Denny who stepped back.

He backed up all the way across the yard to the gate. Zora shot the latch behind him. Tony and Anna were still rolling, of course. Awesome. That was great. What the hell was this cluster going to look like on a TV screen? Camille still sat on the bench, looking small and, suddenly, very old. A blue line stood out on her forehead. Had it always been there?

Felicia had been sitting still during the whole thing in a green wooden Adirondack half-hidden by a jasmine plant that twined up the deck. Was that her ploy? To be as out of the way and forgotten as she could be? It was working.

"Please don't put that in the show."

Felicia smiled sweetly. Too sweetly. "I promise, we'll only use bits that make you look good."

Good and insane, maybe. "The show has to be over. This was a mistake. I can't do this."

"Why don't we talk tomorrow?"

The very request she'd been asking of Denny. "What good would that *do?*" Zora's skin itched along her neck as if she were breaking out in hives, which she probably was.

"How about we chat tomorrow?"

Great, now she was using Zora's own methods against her. "Fine."

In a small voice, Camille said, "How will we pay?"

Zora felt exhaustion flood her bones. Mom wouldn't be able to pay. It was all screwed, well and truly. "It'll be okay, Mom." Her job, now. To soothe Camille.

But she hadn't gotten it right—her voice had been a shade too sharp, and her mother's face crumpled. "I'm so sorry, baby. I'm so sorry—I got confused, and—"

"Seriously, Mom, it'll be okay." She sat down and put her arm around Camille's thin shoulders. "I'll make it work."

"Where will you stay, though?"

Zora gestured at the kitchen. "The laundry room and living room are pretty...damaged. But the kitchen looks fine, and so does the bedroom, so at least I'll have a place to stay while I figure it all out."

Jake's face was drawn. "I'm sorry, Zora, but that's going to be a no-go, at least for a while. Tox Ellis said you can't stay inside."

"Why? It's fine. Look at it. Totally in one piece."

"Building department won't see it that way. They'll red-tag the whole building until the structural repairs are made."

It felt like a punch to the gut. "But...it's my home. Surely they can prop it up and close the hole with boards. Right? That's what I've seen in other places. Or maybe it was on TV. I don't know. But no."

Jake's face was grim. "I wish it wasn't me telling you that."

"What about all my things?"

"He said they'll let you borrow a hard hat and go in when the building department gets here."

Zora thumped onto the porch swing. "Oh, God." It was all starting to sink in. Her mother had no money, only her pension, which went directly to her housing and care. Even though Denny undoubtedly had home insurance, that insurance company would go after her mother. Wouldn't it? If they drew against her pension, she'd lose her place in the care center. Could they do that?

If so, Zora would have to pay for the repairs with her savings (and not use them for a down payment) while finding a new place to live.

Her bones felt made of concrete, her blood made of pumice. She couldn't move. Above her head, Felicia was saying something to Jake, her mother was twittering, Tony and Anna were saying something about lighting, but she understood none of their words.

There went the dream. She could almost hear it whooshing away from her.

A house of her own.

Gone.

When she finally did save up enough again, she'd be priced out of the market. If she wanted a home and roots, she'd have to start over in a new town, far inland, where the distance from the sea drove the prices down to bargains.

Who could live that far from the ocean? It was impossible to imagine.

"Zora?" Felicia's voice was louder than the others. "What do you think?"

"Sorry. What?"

"About Jake's boat."

Zora frowned. "I tuned out, I'm sorry. What are you talking about?"

Jake's eyes were so blue they were almost the color of the sky above his head. "I said you could come stay on my boat."

She blinked. Then, unexpectedly, she laughed. "Pardon me?"

"Hey, don't laugh! She's a nice little thing, more than big enough for two people. You might like it. Waking up on a boat in the middle of a rainstorm is just about the most gorgeous thing there is in the world."

For a second, she considered it, even though she was going to have to cancel the contract. There was no way she could go forward. Oh, God, was there a financial penalty for canceling?

She couldn't remember. She'd remember that, right?

No, she *had* to cancel the contract. Or—could she buy a house with them, and flip it? Would that give her the money she needed? She could rush through the taping, so she could hurry up and resell the house. She could get the money from the sale and do what she needed to do to protect her mother's pension. Quickly. Before the lawyers could complete a lawsuit and garnish her mother's income.

And then she remembered the live-in clause. If she got a house through the show, she had to live in it for a year, ostensibly something about the tax burden for the show. *Damn it.*

"Zora?" Jake's voice brought her to the present. "Want to stay on my boat tonight?"

Cozy below deck, the boat rocking with her tucked safely inside. Where? Did he have a couch? This was a show on which they went on *dates*, not on booty calls, right?

As if he were reading her mind, he said, "I have a pull-out sofa. I'd sleep there, you take the bed."

"Oh, thank you. But no. I've got plenty of friends I can stay with." But really, did she? Adele and Nate had the new baby. Lana and Taft were having their floors done, and they were staying temporarily at the Golden Spike Hotel. Dixie had no room in her trailer—her dog barely fit inside with her. Mom had her apartment in the care home, and while Zora could stay on the roll-out cot, that was restricted to one night a week so that overnighters didn't use too much water.

Felicia tapped her clipboard with a nail. "We'll pay you."

Jake said, "Huh?"

"Pardon me?" Zora said again.

"To live on his boat. On camera. *Big* bonus."

Jake said quickly, "How big? And do I get it, too?"

He was way more on top of what was going on than she was.

"Big enough. I'll talk to production, and we can chat about it tomorrow. But I guarantee we can make it work to make you happy. Stay on board the boat, keep the cameras rolling, and we pay you for your time. Starting tonight. We'll retro your check."

*Damn* it. Zora *needed* that money.

And the chance to make it wouldn't last long, that was for sure. She knew she had to quit the show. She couldn't live in any of those houses for a minute, let alone a year.

So why wasn't she quitting right then? Why wasn't she breaking it to Felicia?

Zora took in a deep breath as she thought. She scuffed her tennis shoes in the gravel that she'd carted onto the path bucket by bucket. She'd bought it at the local quarry and had gotten to know the owner by name.

Every bit of the edging she'd put in by hand, laying the wooden strips down and driving them into the hard-packed soil. There wasn't an inch of the back garden or the front yard that she didn't know, hadn't touched. It had been stupid, she'd known, to do so much work in the garden of a rental. But she'd been there for seven years, ever since she'd started teaching. She'd made it through one landlord (Horace had been the best landlord ever—she'd made him pies with the blackberries that ran wild down in the creek below, and he'd let her paint the rooms whatever color she wanted) and Denny, up to now, while surly, hadn't shown any inclination to make her leave.

That was over.

"Yeah," Jake said slowly. "I'll take that kind of money. Hell, yes. I need it. Zora?"

Her gaze landed on the gate that led to the school. That garden, the one on the other side of that gate, that was the garden of her heart.

"Hey, can I show you something?" She knew her voice sounded weird, but Jake didn't seem to mind.

"Okay."

"Over here." She led her way past the avocado

tree she'd put in, careful to make sure it was the self-propagating kind. It hadn't borne fruit for the first three years. When it did, though—she could make guacamole for the whole town, and at city functions, she often had. It was the best one in town.

She'd be leaving it soon so that it could be rented to vacationers.

A deep ache in her chest started building, and tears wouldn't be far behind.

Everyone was looking at her.

She pushed open the gate and stepped into the garden she'd started on the school grounds. She led Jake through the path that ran between the raised beds. "My kids did all this. All of it. Look at your feet."

Jake looked down at the mulched pathway. "They made this?"

She nodded. "An acacia fell on the other side of the playground last year in that big storm we got. The school let me dump the mulch over here. It took two weeks of moving it by hand. They loved it. They'd move mulch on recess instead of playing four square."

He reached out to touch a broccoli plant that reached up past his shoulder. "It's amazing."

"It's my life."

"You'll still have this, though."

"Yeah." Zora felt like her head were packed

with cotton. "Sure. No matter where I live, I'll still get to come here. But I won't...I won't get to just hop out of bed and wander in here wearing my bathrobe. See the hammock we put up over in the corner? That's my favorite place to read."

Her cat wound around Jake's legs. "Who's this handsome guy?"

"Huh. That's Mr. Prickles. He's not that into men. I wouldn't touch him if I were you."

"Cats love me." He reached down.

Mr. Prickles rubbed his head against Jake's hand. "See?"

Then Mr. Prickles swiped him with an unsheathed paw. Jake held up his hand, bleeding in three places. "You did warn me."

"I did. I should get you a Band-Aid or two."

"Eh." He wiped his hand on his jeans. "So you were saying about the hammock." A smile played on his lips even though he was still bleeding.

"I read there on Saturday mornings. Mr. Prickles lies in there with me. It's heaven."

"Are you still in your bathrobe at this point?"

She nodded. "Yep. Just my bathrobe." It was true. She usually came out after her shower, and the robe was totally decent. She wasn't sure why she was admitting it to him, but it had something to do with the fact that she was about to lose the home she'd loved more than any other, and flirting with him in a completely awkward way was a distraction. "Nothing else."

"I see." His voice was a dark rumble. "Will you bring that to the boat tonight?"

Right. The boat. Stay with him on camera?

Well, why the hell not? It wasn't like they'd catch them doing anything. "Yeah. Maybe it'll rain."

# FIFTEEN

Jake was nervous, which was a strange thing.

It was past nine p.m. already, and Zora still hadn't called out from the dock. She hadn't texted him, though he'd made sure she had his number.

Nerves weren't normal for him. Every once in a while, when he did something crazy, he felt an excitement in his belly, as if his stomach could move of its own volition. A deep, shaky wobble. The first time he'd gone skydiving, as he'd stood at the edge of the airplane door, he'd felt his stomach lurch in an exhilarated way. When he'd been the guy who got to light the big Darling Bay city fireworks on the Fourth of July, he'd felt the same thing as he lit the fuse and ran backward.

This was different. His stomach was rocking like a skiff in a squall.

He wiped his palms on his hands and took a deep sniff.

Damn it, he just couldn't tell. His brothers ribbed him all the time about how his boat smelled like a wet dog. The boat retained moisture, that was for sure. His clothes, especially the ones in deep storage, probably did smell musty all the time. But that was another reason he favored using the clothesline out on deck. Sun made things smell good.

He'd burned some incense an old girlfriend had left him (the scent of her had lasted a whole lot longer than their relationship) and made some coffee, just because fresh coffee always smelled good, right? He'd changed the sheets on his bed, and he'd ostentatiously left fresh bedding on the sofa so she'd know that he meant to keep to his word—he'd sleep out here. He always had liked stretching out on the extra-long couch with its extra-firm cushions.

Of course, he loved just about everything in this place. That's probably why he'd never gotten out of the slip for more than a couple of nights at a time— he was always on the verge of making it completely perfect. There was always just one more touch to add.

"Crap." He burned his lips on the coffee he'd

poured absentmindedly. Usually coffee didn't keep him awake, ever. He rose early and worked hard, and he normally fell asleep when his head hit the pillow. But the combination of a belly full of caffeine and his first love sleeping on board?

He hated it when he couldn't sleep. He poured out the cup.

He peeked out the window. Still nothing.

For a few moments, he was up top inspecting his lines, the knots that were as secure as they always were.

No sign of her.

Could they tell he was nervous?

Of course, Jake didn't know who "they" were. He had no idea who was watching the videos from the cameras they'd installed. Should have asked—why hadn't that occurred to him? He imagined a clandestine van parked just past the river, maybe by the gazebo, filled with two hairy men who chugged Mountain Dew while leaning forward, fascinated by and evaluating his every move. More likely, though, they had the cameras pipe into somewhere nine hours south in L.A., monitored by an intern whose job it was to send on the bits that were actually interesting.

Then, it came.

Her whistle. A middle-pitched note followed by a rapid swoop up to a high-pitched one. *Whoo-hoot.*

And so much came back to him, a flood tide of memories he'd stored so far back they didn't even exist until that moment.

Her whistle from the front of Bill's property.

Her whistle in the halls at school when they passed each other between classes.

Her long, low, happy whistle after the first time they made love. It had always been unexpected and such a startlingly clear, sweet noise, like a happy bird trying out a cushy nest for the first time.

The sound brought all of it back. And he got more nervous, his stomach banging against his lungs as if it wanted out.

He went up on deck.

She looked amazing, as usual, and he could tell she hadn't gone to any trouble. She'd washed off all the set makeup, thank God. She just looked like Zora, fresh eyes, curved cheeks, breasts that swayed slightly under her sweatshirt as she reached forward to take hold of the line at the bow.

"Hey, there!" Oh, Lord, had his voice actually broken with a squeak like he hadn't heard since high school? Awesome. "Glad you're here. Come aboard."

She smiled. Was it at his vocal embarrassment or just a friendly grin?

"Thanks," she said quickly. He couldn't remember ever seeing her on board a boat, and that was proven in a moment as she rocked back on her heels.

"Whoa," she said. "Sorry, not used to this. Pretty rough waters tonight, huh?"

The water was almost glass tonight, the boat moving the slightest bit, mostly with the motion of her boarding. "Sure. You good?"

"I'm good." She paused. "Are you *sure* this thing won't sink while I'm on it?"

"I'm really, really sure." Hell, if a hurricane roared unexpectedly through tonight, he'd hold the boat together with his bare hands to keep her safe.

"So no sharks will get me?"

"No sharks, I promise."

Zora put her hands on her hips and turned around slowly. He tried to use his imagination to see what she was seeing for the first time. The lights of the marina, sparkling on three sides of them. To the northwest was the channel in the bay that led to open ocean and rough waters most of the time. Metal clanged on masts all around them, and Jake could hear the sound of Steely Dan coming from Terry Dunlap's boat.

"I like that song," she said. "It's friendly here, huh? You can hear everything?"

Jake nodded. "Steely Dan means Terry and his wife are getting busy."

"Oh!"

Why had he said it? Way to bring sex right into it, when it was, really, the thing he was trying hardest not to think about. It was honestly kind of hard not to, though, with her standing right there in front of him, looking not much older than she had when they'd dated in high school. Her round cheeks had filled out a bit, charmingly so, and the swell of her breasts was fuller. Her hips were wider, and for a full second, he battled the image of putting his hands on either hip, pulling her to him.

He was going insane.

Old friend. Okay, old girlfriend. Staying with him out of necessity, on camera.

No big deal.

Why, then, did he offer his hand to help her make her way down the ladder onto the lower deck? She was able-bodied and strong, and she'd gained her footing. She didn't need his hand.

Nor did she take it. "I'm good." She found the stair rail and followed him down.

And Jake got more nervous, his insides clanging like a nautical bell. He'd tidied the best he could, and it still looked messy.

"Please disregard the mess. Last-minute and everything."

"Mess? Seriously?" She twirled again. "If you think this is messy, you should never come to my house. Also, there's half a car in the middle of the living room, so it's a little worse than normal, but I'm kind of a slob."

He'd only gone around the house earlier, not inside it. "Slob as in hoarder in training? As many piles? As in tidy but dirty? Or dirty but tidy?"

Zora gave him a curious look. "Slob as in dirty dishes in the sink, but laundry is always put away."

"So a four on the scale of slob."

She nodded. "A four if this is a one. I'd call this neat as a pin, although what does that mean, anyway? Why are pins neater than anything else?"

He remembered this, her nervous chatter. It made him feel a little better. He wasn't the only nervous one. "Okay, so let me show you your berth." She followed him into the master stateroom, which had dark panels that he'd put in himself and a deep blue down duvet. The skylight over the bed was one of his favorite things about the *Kerplunk* (although it did sometimes leak during heavy rain. That was a pain in the ass).

"I can't take this," she said. "I'll sleep on the couch."

It hit him then, what they were doing. They were going to be their best selves, polite and cordial as hell for the sake of the show and the cameras and the audience.

That was probably a good idea.

But it wasn't the only idea.

"Hey, sit down." Jake gestured to the bed. Was this weird? Yeah, it was. He could see it in her eyes.

But she climbed up on the bed anyway. He did, too, careful not to get too close to her. She was spooked, and he didn't want her to bolt.

"What if we tried something?"

Zora briefly bit her bottom lip. "Try what?"

"Let's just be totally honest with each other."

She blinked. "Um. What do you mean?"

"Like, let's try throwing out all the politeness and the not-stepping-on-toes and the saying the things that we know we're supposed to say. Like you saying that you should take the couch when we both know it's easier for me to sleep there since I'm used to being on the boat at night, and you're not. Plus, there's a door you can close, and that'll help you sleep easier."

"But I don't want to tell you every single thing I think."

"Hell, no, we shouldn't do *that*." Then he'd have to tell her how her hair looked like elm wood, light strands mixed with darker ones, and he'd have to tell her how her whistle had affected him from the soles of his feet upward. "I just mean we don't play the polite game. Ever. You tell me what you want, and I'll tell you what I want. Within reason. We won't just buy into the idea that since we're on camera we have to be as good a human being that's ever lived."

Zora tilted her chin. "I don't think that reality shows are really known for this kind of good behavior, do you?"

"Some aren't, sure. But *On The Market* isn't a housewives show, you know? We're known for being good brothers. We say the right thing, and we try not to screw up too much on camera."

"What about when you and that redhead got lost when you rode horses to the beach?"

Zora watched the show? That made him both happy and embarrassed. "It wasn't a rattler, that's all I can tell you. Editing got hold of that, and they inserted that sound."

"And that kiss while said rattler was ostensibly at your feet?"

"Nothing at our feet but sand."

"Good, because the world thought you were an idiot."

His stomach did a long, slow dive as she smiled at him, taking the sting out of her words. "I was one, honestly." Why had he spent any time kissing the redhead, whose name completely escaped him right now, when Zora had been in town, just around the corner?

Zora smiled, and Jake felt something relax inside him. She said, "Okay. So we don't bullshit each other. Does that mean we can swear on tape, like I just did?"

"Fuck, yes. They do the editing. Not us."

She grinned. "Where *are* the cameras, anyway?"

"I haven't been able to find them. They came in here without me—"

Looking startled, she said, "With your permission?"

"Of course. Really, they're not out to get us, I promise. They're not out to humiliate us. This is, as reality shows go, a pretty tame one, I think. We fix up houses, we go on dates, occasionally we fall..."

"In love."

Jake nodded.

"Have you ever?" she asked.

Ever what? Fallen in love? Of course. First of all —maybe most of all—with her, all those years ago. "You mean on camera?"

"Yeah."

"No."

"I'm saying. The redhead—I can't remember her name—"

He finally remembered. "Diana."

"That's it. You and she looked pretty happy together as the credits rolled."

"She had a boyfriend in Denver."

Zora drew her knees under her on the bed so

that she was kneeling, eager. "You're *kidding* me. Tell me everything."

"She was doing it for the exposure for her online embroidery company."

"Did Felicia know that? Going in?"

He knew there was no way they'd air this footage now, which was a good feeling. "No way. Felicia is all about the show, and I get how she's pretty overbearing when she's with us, but she has our best interests at heart. If I fell in love and the show ended, I think she'd be fine with it, as long as I was actually happy."

"Yeah." Zora touched her lip the way she always had, as if she were barely holding herself back from *bbbbbbbbb*ing it. "You're the last man still standing."

Jake rubbed the back of his neck and without thinking, flopped back onto his pillow. He and Zora were now only an inch or two apart. He could feel the heat of her, and for a crazy moment, he wanted to roll in her direction onto his side, until her kneecaps pressed into his chest.

Instead, he just kept his eyes on the ceiling. "Yep. Last one standing."

# SIXTEEN

Zora couldn't believe where she was. On his bed, on his boat.

*Jake's* bed. *Jake's* boat.

Just a few years ago, Molly Darling had tried to talk her around one time. *He's a sweetie. You're friends with everyone in town. Be nice to him. You'll be friendly someday. He's not a bad guy.*

And here she was, being reminded again that he wasn't that bad a guy.

He wasn't bad at all.

He'd just been such a reminder of an awful time—he'd gotten the flavor, the stink of it all over him in her memories. "You're kind of all right, aren't you?"

He snorted. "You sound so surprised."

"It's just that I always thought you were such a dick."

"*Why?*"

"It's just what I told myself about you. What if I've always been wrong about you, and we could have been friends this whole time?" She paused, surprise flooding her chest. "Whoa, you're right. It does feel good to say what I think."

"So you told yourself I was an ass? For that long? Why?"

Zora looked down at the blue bedspread. She tugged a stray thread, willing it to break. Instead, it puckered the fabric, so she let it go and smoothed it back out. "Because. You know."

"I know what?"

She flapped a ridiculous hand between them. "Because of what happened. Between us." What if they *did* clear the air? What if Zora told him the truth and let go of the resentment she'd held toward him for so long, resentment that she could barely fan to life anymore. The heat had gone out of it so long ago that some days she could barely remember what she was angry about.

"You broke up with me," he said. "And you never told me why."

"I *did.*" But she hadn't. She'd said she couldn't be with him. Hadn't that been reason enough?

Shouldn't that be good enough for someone? "We were kids, anyway."

"I know." He sighed and closed his eyes. "It was a long time ago. Water under the bridge."

That was another cliché she'd rested on back then. It didn't matter because it was water under the bridge. It didn't matter if he were the last man on earth. "Yeah."

"So." His eyes were still closed. "Do you still think I'm a dick?"

She paused. "Well, I hadn't really thought—"

He popped up, coming onto his side, suddenly two or three inches closer to her. She could feel his radiant body heat on her knees, so she slid backward. The bed itself was no bigger than a full and not really made to hold two grown people having a conversation.

"Hey," he said. "Remember what we agreed?"

Zora pulled at a ragged cuticle. "Oh, yeah."

"So. Do you still think that about me?"

"Not today."

He gave a surprised laugh. "That's pretty good. Not today. But tomorrow?"

"Unclear," she admitted.

"Okay, then. That's fair enough. I can work with that."

Oh, man, he sure could. With those dreamy, bedroom eyes that always looked brilliant at the deep-blue middle and the tiniest bit sad at the outer, darker edges, he could probably work with anything.

Whew, the bedroom was *hot*, wasn't it? She dabbed at sweat rising on her temple.

Maybe he noticed—which was embarrassing—because he got on his knees and reached for a handle. "Here's how you open the portholes. Getting the cross-breeze is nice. Nothing better than the smell of the tide turning in the darkness."

Her own stomach swayed along with the boat. *Darkness*. With him, just feet away, on the other side of a thin piece of wood.

And the whole nation watching.

No.

This was impossible. What was she doing here?

"Jake, while we're telling the truth—I completely hated all three of those houses. I know you're disappointed, and we didn't get any chance to talk about house number three, but I'm sure you heard the comments I was making to people like Felicia and Anna. It's absolutely, one-hundred percent—"

"Not you," he finished.

"Was it that obvious?"

"Pretty damn clear, yes. You looked like you were going to cry when you saw the marble countertop."

"Why? Why can't *one* newer house have old tile on the countertops? What about the old green tile like my rental kitchen has?"

"You loved living in that place." His voice was soft.

Zora nodded, ignoring the salt in the back of her throat. It wasn't worth crying about—the wrecked house that she'd use her savings to fix, Denny's anger, her mother's carelessness with both her insurance and her life. At least Camille was okay. "It could have been so much worse. What if she'd been hurt? Or killed? My place doesn't matter at all, does it?"

He shook his head. "I guess not."

"You know I'm going to have to leave the show." It hurt almost physically to say, right in the middle of her chest.

"You can't. I don't want to do it without you."

Something pulled between them then. A tug, a heaviness that made her want to sway toward him. The feeling was recognizable, like a scent she hadn't smelled in years, one that transported her backward in time.

"The contract says I have to pick one of the three houses."

"We can change it."

"Has the show ever done that?"

Jake gave a slow nod then a shake of his head.

"No. I don't know. Probably not, but there's an exception for every rule, right?"

His eyes met hers.

Her rule had been staying out of his way for the rest of her natural-born life.

Rules had exceptions.

Neither of them spoke. Something moved between them, something electrical and super-heated.

Zora's heart rate launched into the triple digits, and she stood, almost hitting her head on a small shelf full of books. "Bathroom?" she said.

He blinked. "Oh, yeah. Let me show you how it works."

"Then I think it's bedtime. For me. I mean, I'm sleepy." Through her babbling, she tried to fake a yawn, but it came out like a garbled noise old Mr. Prickles might make (she'd left him with her neighbor). She scrambled in the bag she'd hastily packed in her house, that had smelled like gasoline and singed hair, and came out with her toothbrush and toothpaste. "Yep. Brush my teeth. *That's* what I'm going to do."

Thank God, Jake didn't take the opportunity to make fun of her. "Right here." He opened a small door in the passageway that she hadn't even noticed before. The minuscule room didn't look like it would hold a sneeze, but inside were a tiny metal sink, a metal toilet, and a shower head overhead right between the two. Jake opened the cabinet behind the small mirror. "Everything you need in here, Band-Aids, Tylenol, you know. Water's not potable so don't drink it, but it's fine for brushing your teeth. It's a wet room, so to take a shower just shut the toilet lid and let everything get wet."

She didn't ask what she'd do with a towel, how to keep that dry. Would she hang it on the outside door latch? Reach out naked to get it? That was a firm nope. She'd shower at Mom's or at Tuesday's house.

"Okay." Jake stepped toward her.

Zora stepped back but ran smack into the wall behind her. Now would be the time to step to the right and allow him out of the bathroom, to let him go down the corridor.

But she didn't. She froze, but it wasn't cold that made her go still. It was something like heat, that electric feeling again that might just spill right through her—a buzz that would make her do something she'd regret, like kissing him or something even worse.

He went perfectly still, too.

Time stopped being measured by seconds and began moving through her body in heartbeats. One heartbeat, the sound of a breath caught and held. Two heartbeats, his blue eyes darkening. Three, his scent rising, like ocean and deodorant and something darker. Four, then five, and six.

Still, neither of them moved.

It was too long—*too long*. One of them had to break this gaze and the spell that came with it, a spell that took Zora right back to the time when he'd been everything to her, when he'd been hers and she was his, and that was all that mattered.

When he spoke, his voice was low and hoarse. "I thought you'd be married by now. House. Kids. Picket fence."

Her pulse beat like a rabbit's. "Yeah, well. I thought you'd be sailing around the world for the second time by now, kids hanging off the sides of the boat." Neither of them mentioned husbands or wives. Neither of them had to.

Stubble was thick on Jake's wide jaw. "Huh. I guess we're both waiting for the right time."

Every cell in her body told her to stay in place, that if she did, she'd be rewarded by him taking the final half-step to press his body against her and catch her mouth with his, hot and needy and everything her body was screaming for.

But the sound of her bag falling off the bed broke the spell.

She scuttled left. "Sorry."

"Yeah. Um." He cleared his throat and stepped to her right. Two more steps and he was back in the galley. He opened a small fridge. "Okay, then. Um. I'm going to have a beer on deck before bed. You want one?"

"No, thanks," she squeaked and dove into the bathroom, closing the door behind her.

In the mirror, her eyes looked glassy, her color high. Even her pupils were dilated.

It wasn't *fair* that he could make her feel like this, just by one stupid look. She shouldn't be here —she needed to quit the show first thing in the morning and find another place to stay.

She brushed her teeth and thanked her lucky stars that bathrooms were the only guaranteed off-camera spaces while she was on the show.

God, when she'd been in the hallway, she'd forgotten the cameras altogether. They'd caught that on camera. What would it look like? A frozen moment of awkwardness?

That might have been it, honestly. Maybe he hadn't noticed the heat—

No, that was crap. They could have melted sand between them, like a strike of lightning hitting a beach.

There was a gentle rap on the door. "Zora, I forgot to tell you something."

Oh, sure. That was what he was going to lead with? A spark of joy bloomed in her, and she pulled the door open too eagerly.

"Mmmm?" She tried to lean sexily against the door, unsure exactly how to pull that off.

Instead of planting a kiss on her, though, as she'd expected, he merely pointed behind her. "Toilet paper's there. Under that plastic cover."

"Oh. Thanks." She pulled her sexy hip back into place.

"It's to keep the shower water off it."

That was obvious.

He was still standing so close.

Too close.

He cleared his throat. "And one other thing."

It would be about where to hang the towel. Something prosaic. Something—

He came at her fast, pushing her against the sink.

# SEVENTEEN

The spark leaped between their lips again but there was no time for Jake to comment on the zap—he was too busy kissing her, and she seemed to be pretty busy kissing him back.

She tasted like heaven, like sweet and salt.

He couldn't breathe correctly when his lips were touching hers—it was as though his lungs forgot how to work, but that was okay because she was pushing back against him, pressing the air and heat and lust back to him. It was impossible to get enough of her—he kissed her even harder, taking life and sustenance and just enough oxygen to keep doing this, the thing he wanted to do for the rest of his life.

Yeah. He wanted to kiss her forever.

Zora made a noise against his mouth, though, that made him instantly forget about kissing her and drove his brain to the next stop on this ride of need.

He drew back, trying desperately to find the emergency brake in case he had to pull it.

But she said, "Please don't stop. *Please* don't stop." Then she wrapped her arms around his neck, pressed her breasts against his chest, and he was lost again, drowning in the sea of her, happy to die exactly this way.

"Bed," she mumbled against his mouth. "Bed."

Then they were in the stateroom, stumbling against the bench. He lifted her shirt over her head and just stared. A light pink bra—he remembered the first time he'd ever seen that pale color against her breasts, and he felt like an eighteen-year-old all over again. Then her jeans came off, all four of their hands working to make it happen. Jake stripped off his T-shirt, and for the most adorable second, she leaned her head against his chest and giggled.

They were eighteen. And it was also fourteen years later, and they were grown up, and the most beautiful woman in the world was giggling with her forehead pressed against his heart, the heart that might burst right open out of happiness.

But he had to be sure—he lifted her chin with his finger. "Are you sure?" He didn't even know why she'd hated him for so long. Was she going to regret this?

"I'm *so* sure." She helped him then with his jeans, and his underwear, and then he stood naked in front of her, hard as hell and twice as hot.

Zora touched him, and he jerked, moaning. "Lord, woman. Easy, there."

Then she screamed.

She screamed like he'd pinched her—which he decidedly hadn't—and she leaped into the bed, scrabbling for the duvet and pulling it over her desperately.

"What the *hell?*" But it hit him as he said it—*the cameras.* "SHIT." He dove under the covers with her.

Jake didn't know what he expected, but it wasn't what she did next.

Zora, still completely under the duvet, started howling with laughter. It was completely dark under the sheet and duvet, visibility zero, but her laugh was so lighthouse-intense it almost lit the interior of the bed. He reached for her, and she reached for him at the same time.

"Did they see us?" Her laughter was as contagious as her heat.

"Probably."

"Oh, well." There was nothing but joy in her voice as she pressed herself against him. "Let's just stay under here forever. Let's not let any part of us stick out of the covers. Maybe the room mics won't even pick up any noise. Let's just stay here."

"Yes." Yes, yes, yes. He would stay with her here forever. They wouldn't have to eat or drink. They'd just stay inside her heat. Her lips were wet and slick against his, and he felt both of their bodies break into a sweat, and he didn't care—he just wanted more. They were pressed face to face, and his cock felt her heat. She tilted her hips, and he almost lost it, right there.

Because he wasn't a teenager anymore and hopefully less prone to losing it, he moved and slid his hand down her side, cupping her breast and catching her nipple between his fingers and twisting lightly. She moaned, her lips now against his ear. He'd been hard before. Now he was made of iron, hard and hot and *needing*.

With his mouth still sucking her nipple, teasing it, licking and biting, his hand started drifting down, toward the center of her heat, where she throbbed.

She laughed out loud and then gasped. "More, more."

He whispered, "You sure?"

"Hell, yes," she said. "Please, you have to...."

Jake didn't *get* it. She was put together like a regular woman. She had two arms, two legs, and all the normal parts that came with being a human, as far as he could tell. He was enjoying checking. But as he slipped a finger inside her heat, he knew that no one had ever felt like this before, that no woman had ever been this tight and slippery, and at the same time, no woman had ever been this much fucking fun.

Because she was still laughing in his ear. Laughing as if she was having as insanely wonderful a time as he was. *Happiness.* That was inside his chest.

The rest of his body, though, held so much lust he could barely keep from plunging into her wet heat with his cock. *Hold back, there.* Keeping his fingers inside her, he trailed his tongue down her body, taking his time, licking and teasing each sensitive point he found, her waist, her hip, the inside of her thigh. It was an inferno under the covers—sweat rolled off him, and every inch of her skin was wet, too.

She'd stopped laughing and was tensing around his hand. She gave a low groan as he lowered his mouth to her, pressing his tongue against her clit, hard and round under his lips. He licked her, keeping up a steady rhythm, while his fingers kept up their motion until she writhed under his mouth and hand, her hands wrapped his hair, pressing him into her, her voice above him, begging him never, ever to stop.

And when she'd stopped pulsing around him, when she purred and pulled him up her slippery body, laughing, he gapped the covers and took a breath of cool air.

"We need—hurry—we need—"

"Right here." Yes, the cameras would see his arm whapping around into the bedside table to grab the condom. And he didn't give a shit about anything but her, about how he needed her, and *only* her.

Back under the covers, he slipped on the condom with her eager fingers helping.

And when she finally wrapped her legs around him and he pushed into her, it was as if they'd never been apart.

She gasped against him, rocking against him in perfect rhythm. His cock found purchase and friction, heat and speed, and oh Christ, she was so fucking wet, and she screamed into his mouth, and then he came, and she did too, and it wasn't like anything else—she was with him again.

Finally.

With huge gasps, they tossed the covers off their heads. Jake pushed off the duvet—he should have done that first—and shoved the sheet down to his navel.

"Unfair," she said. I don't get to do that."

He could still barely breathe. "It's *totally* unfair.

No one wants to look at my chest, but the whole world would want to gaze at yours." He lifted the sheet a bit. Her breasts were luscious, full, and round, her nipples softening now. He grazed one with his thumb, and she panted a little, her tongue soft and pink and perfect. The sound of her breath went right to his head, and his heart did a somersault. She closed her eyes and scooted so that her head was resting on his shoulder.

"I missed you." The words shocked him as they escaped his lips, but he knew they were true, and they were out there. So he doubled down. "I didn't know that I missed you, but I sure as hell did."

"Mmmm." She snuggled close and pressed a kiss to his neck. "I..."

"You," he prompted.

She whispered in his ear, "I missed you, too."

EIGHTEEN

In the morning, he was gone. There was a Post-it stuck to the (still mostly full) coffeepot that said: *Aidan needed help. Meet at your place at 9? Felicia wants to film.*

All business. Except for the little heart scratched under the words. Her heart sped up.

Business, think about business. That was the important part.

*Was it?* The night before—oh, Lord.

She'd *slept* with him. What's more, she'd wanted it. She'd have done anything for it last night. Even with everything that had happened so long ago—and he knew none of it—she'd lost her mind the night before.

And what's more, if he walked right back in here? She'd lose her mind all over again. Zora's forehead started sweating at the very thought of seeing him again.

*Start the day.* She took her toothbrush and toothpaste from her overnight bag and grabbed the towel that Jake had left folded for her at the end of the bed. The whole room, she realized, smelled like sex—their sex. She shivered deliciously and refused to think about the cameras. She showered and changed into a clean shirt and pulled on yesterday's jeans and sweatshirt, and then she carried a mug of coffee up to the deck. The fog was still thick, the summer sun not yet able to burn through it.

And then, trying to forget about Jake and the crazy way she'd felt last night, she looked around.

What a place to *live*.

The *Kerplunk* was moored at the last dock of the marina. It had a perfect view of the other boats bobbing against their bumpers as well as a clear view right into the wide bay. A line of pelicans swooped low over the water, only rising into the air to clear the boats that were heading out the channel to the ocean. The air smelled of seaweed and, faintly, of bacon being cooked in someone's galley. She could hear the strains of someone's guitar. To her right, on a wooden sailboat with peeling green paint, a man was connecting a sail to the lower part of the mast. The man glanced at her and shot her a cheerful smile before going back to working with his knots.

To her left was a new-looking boat—bright, shiny pink with orange letters emblazoned on it. *Night Moves.* As Zora settled into the cushioned seat and took her first few sips, a woman came above deck. Oh, God, it was Mallory.

"Yoohoo!" Mallory trilled, her fingers a blur of waggling. "Zora, is that *you?*" She wore a light-weight white wrap around a bright red bikini top and tight blue pants that dipped low in front, showing off her magnificent abs. She matched her boat perfectly, sexy and sleek.

"Yep," said Zora, unsure of what the protocol was in conversing between boats. Was it manda-tory? Or could she say two words and then bolt back inside? She'd actually never found jewelry-designer Mallory annoyingly perfect until she'd dated Jake. They'd been a jaw-droppingly gorgeous couple for the few months they were together. His TV-ready rugged good looks next to her toothpaste-gleam and blonde, girl-next-door sweetness looked amazing when they breezed through the Golden Spike Cafe, ordering full-fat mochas and the big-gest, sweetest muffins Molly Darling made.

"You're *there!* On Jake's *boat.*" Mallory seemed honestly puzzled. "But *why?*"

"What?"

"I mean, honey. I don't get it." Mallory's forehead, clearly line-free even at twenty-five feet away, furrowed. Then just as quickly, it cleared. "Oh, *I* know. I heard all about it. Your mom ran into your house, and you've been evicted, so I guess you're staying with Jake? What a sweetie he is, right?"

Ouch. Someone like Mallory couldn't even imagine that someone as normal-looking as Zora would grab the interest of someone like Jake. And honestly, would Zora have? If they hadn't had chemistry established already, she probably wouldn't be on the show—wouldn't be in his life.

"You got that right." Shit.

"Aw, that's just *so* like Jake, right?" Her smile was pure sugar. "Once he found a pile of puppies behind a log when we were hiking, and he took them home and nursed them with a bottle for weeks. Like, he was up every two hours with them! Not me, of course. I said, honey, you brought 'em home, they're yours."

Now she was comparing Zora to a stray dog. "Uh-huh."

"Anyone else would have dumped them at the pound. He's such a sucker for the problem cases."

It hurt to be inside Zora's body, waiting for Mallory to realize what she'd just said. Her skin prickled, and her brain filled with white static.

But Mallory didn't seem to notice. She probably wasn't even being passive aggressive. Everyone said Mallory was sweet, just a little man-obsessed.

"He'll probably get over it when he finally sails away forever. Can't take a load of puppies out to sea, huh? Okay, hon! Good seeing you! I need to be at the shop soon, so you come by and say hi sometime, okay? We can grab a coffee or a snack! It's been too long!"

Too long? Zora couldn't remember one time she'd ever hung out one-on-one with Mallory. For a long time after Mallory moved to town, Zora noticed she couldn't ever remember Zora's name. The third time they were introduced, it finally seemed to stick. "You bet," she said weakly.

"Oh, and can you tell Jake I've got his jacket over here? It's just so warm I keep forgetting to return it." With a wink and a dramatic swoop of her white coverup, she disappeared down her steps.

*Mallory* was Jake's type. Not Zora. Mallory had his jacket—what did that mean? Were they dating again?

For Pete's sake, what was Zora doing, messing with him? Things had gone wrong, yes, but Jake himself had always had a good heart—Zora knew that. But his heart was the only one that had ever smashed Zora's into a million pieces.

Jake would always be a little too dangerous for

her blood. (Not last night. Last night he'd been *exactly* dangerous enough.) But soon, he'd sail into the sunset, literally. He'd set out westward and not come back. Maybe with Mallory.

Zora needed to get the hell off the show.

# NINETEEN

Zora's rental house must have been the cutest thing before the car wrecked it. Jake stepped over the pieces of what had obviously been a white gate. The car had been towed out at some point during the night, and where it had stuck out of the house, plywood boards now neatly covered the hole.

Felicia had apparently been watching for him from the open side door that led to the kitchen, thankfully spared. "Code compliance came by. Did you see Aidan at the office? It's not a red tag, thank God. The car drove right into the only part of the wall that was non-load bearing and full of windows, which is why it was such a spectacular mess. Overall, though, it's going to be mostly cosmetic. She should be able to move back in within a month."

"Good. I'm glad." And he was, but there was still the fact that Zora didn't want to be on the show. Would what happened between them the night before help change her mind?

Or would it make her resolve more firm?

Jake stopped on the walkway and held up a donut bag. "I got your favorite. Want to wait out here with me?" *Hang on.* "You've been inside?" he asked. Was it weird that Felicia had gone into the house without Zora there?

A tiny flash of guilt showed in Felicia's face. "I suppose you're right. Come on, crew, let's get out till she gets here."

The *crew* was in there?

"Just getting background cuts. You know."

"What, you want to show viewers where she really came from? Are you going to say she's been living in a smashed hovel? That doesn't sound too fair, does it?"

"What's not fair?" Zora's voice, clear and light.

Jake swore it sounded like music. That was a leftover from last night—from last night's amazingness. He was at the job now, and she was going to quit. And while Felicia freaked out—which she would—he'd have to convince Zora of the truth: that show or no show, he *really* wanted to keep dating her.

On air, or off.

He grinned at her, hoping to share a knowing gaze with her. One that said, *I know how you sound when you laugh in the middle of coming.*

But she didn't meet his gaze. Her face was worried, her lips tight.

Felicia said, "Nothing, actually. I'm quite pleased with the way things are working out, and I want to share it with both of you. Mic packs, please!"

Anna scurried forward and attached a pack to the back of Zora's shirt and then to his.

Zora said, "Felicia, I really have to talk to you. It'll be better to do this off-camera."

"Oh, no." Felicia flipped a few pages on her clipboard and then set it down on top of an empty bird bath. She took a hasty sip of her coffee. "We're filming all of this because I want you on camera for what I have to offer you."

"Fine. But I quit. I'm sorry that I have to do this, so sorry to you and the crew and to you..." She looked right at Jake then, and his stomach fell into his boots. "But I've got a lot of repairs to do. I'm not insured for it, so I'm going to have to use the money I'd saved for a down payment to do it, and then find myself another place to live. I *can't* be on the show." Her voice trembled on the last word.

"Zora." Jake wanted to go to her, but she shook her head firmly as if to warn him off.

"And I'm *fine*. I've always been fine, and I'll continue to be fine. This is the way things are supposed to go. It is what it is. I do apologize to the cast and crew for wasting your time, Felicia."

Felicia, though, instead of reacting to what Zora had just said, ushered them onto a bench just big enough for both of them. It was a little cozy, in fact, and Jake's thigh touched Zora's. Just that light warmth brought back a flash of what she'd felt like underneath him last night, under the covers, moving like she was born to be there, with him.

He cleared his throat. "What's this all about?"

Felicia pulled up a metal chair and perched on the edge. "Tony? Levels good?"

Tony, holding one of the cameras that swung around them, shot her a thumbs-up.

"Okay. Hold the levels but quit filming for a minute, okay?"

Tony looked as confused as Jake felt.

Felicia leaned forward. "Zora. Jake. We at *On the Market* have an unconventional offer for you."

"Oh, no," said Jake. Some of the seasons had had twists. He'd date one girl, but it was her best friend who actually wanted the house. Or the chosen house would suddenly be found to be falling down from termites, but that fact was only "just then" coming to light. Fake tension added for viewing spice.

Felicia shook her head. "It's a good thing. Zora, what if you could keep this cottage?"

Zora snorted. "I can't. So whatever it is, it's not that. What are you proposing?"

"Your landlord wants to sell."

"Someday, probably."

"We talked to him this morning. He's already signing papers that Liam is drawing up."

Jake felt, rather than saw, her shock. Her body went rigid. "What?"

"He's decided he'd like to sell. That is, he'd like to sell, but only to you."

Zora shook her head again. "I don't think you're hearing what I'm saying. I *do not have the money*."

Felicia said, "It's true, he's asking an awful lot more than this trashed cottage is worth. But he can do that, and we can pay him."

It clicked. Jake got it, and something inside him fell. The show was great, but it had its own best interests at heart, not theirs. "You've got to be putting a *hell* of a lot of bait on this line. What's the catch?"

Felicia narrowed her eyes. "Not that big a deal. Just something that we've never done on the show."

Oh, God. "You want to play last night on air."

Zora came to life. "No! No, no, no, are you *kidding* me? What do you have, heat-sensing cameras?"

"No, of course, not. You were covered by the

sheet." Felicia's gaze fell to her lap, and Jake could see that she was nervous, too. That was something—Felicia was usually the unflappable one. She went on, "Our techs might have *heard* it all, of course. We'll lose the naked part of the footage out of respect."

Yeah, right. Were they supposed to feel grateful for that?

Zora's voice was low. "How *much* did they hear?"

Felicia raised her eyes but trained them on the roofline above them. "Enough to know that you two are a perfect match, especially when you rock the boat."

"Felicia!" Jake clamped his hands to his thighs to keep himself in the seat. "Are you *blackmailing* us?"

"Oh, darlings, *no*! Quite the opposite. We're offering you something huge because we want to make you both happy."

He lowered his voice to a growl. "Tell us now."

"We want you to get married on camera."

# TWENTY

It wasn't really relief that lit the front of Zora's mind bright white—it was something else. Humor? Hilarity? Maybe it was hysteria, a sudden gut-wrenching bout of it. "Married? Oh, my God, Felicia, I thought you were being serious. This is just about me trying to get off the show, right? I'll help you find someone else, I promise. I have two girlfriends at school who've also been thinking about buying. Jake, both of them are cute and sweet, and"—oh, crap, it *did* hurt to think about setting him up with someone else—"I think you know Lisa already?"

But Jake's eyes were stunned, wide like he'd been slapped on the back of the head. "Felicia's serious."

Zora laughed. "No, she's not."

"Look at her."

Felicia was sitting very still, watching both of them. Her face was relaxed—the only sign of tension the way she held the clipboard so tightly that her knuckles were white. "We're dead serious."

"*Why?*" Zora wanted to pull up her legs and wrap her arms around her knees. As a teen she sat like that, her sweatshirt lifted and pulled down around her legs so that she was in a cocoon. The sweatshirt she wore today wouldn't hold both her and her bent legs, but she wished it would. "Why would you even offer this?"

Slowly, Jake said, "Because it'll get the ratings she's looking for. A wedding will pull in all the viewers we lost with that terrible seventh season."

Zora hadn't watched that one, but she knew the contestant—Zora would choose cleaning out all the lint dryers at the local laundromat over having to watch Nelly dither about paint choices. She was, perhaps, the most boring woman in the world. Even thinking about her made Zora a little sleepy.

But the current situation woke her right back up. "You mean, I'd get the cottage. This house."

Felicia smiled. "This very one."

"Fixed."

"From top to bottom, exactly the way you want it."

"I'd just have to bring my down payment."

"That's right. We'd fix the house, gratis. You'd be responsible for the mortgage, nothing more."

"It would be *mine*." The last word escaped her on a breath. Her house.

It could be hers. The raspberry canes. The jasmine that twined over the edge of the porch. The asparagus that only gave a few spears each year, but they were so perfect that she kept their spot pristine and clear, ready for early spring.

And the gate that led to her student garden with its hammock and its wonderfully crooked mulched paths. It would be *her* gate. Her own gate!

Something else occurred to her. "I could change things? Like change the light fixture in the living room?" It was a horrible green glass monstrosity that she detested.

Felicia laughed. "That would be least of the changes you could make. We could add another bedroom. Another half-bath. Whatever you want."

It felt stunning, like her hands were suddenly full of diamonds.

A home for her.

Jake leaned forward. "Let's go back to that wedding thing."

"Yes. It would be the Ballard Brothers wedding show. Guaranteed to get the highest ratings of all time for the show. Nothing like a wedding to pull in the entire heartland."

"But..." Jake's voice trailed off as his eyes found hers. "But we're not..."

"We're not in love," said Zora briskly. If he couldn't say it, she could. "I know TV is fake, but wouldn't that be taking fake way past its limit?"

Felicia held up a finger and then moved to drag a chair near to the bench. She sat. "This is a big thing to think about, I know, so let's really dialogue about it."

Zora hated it when people used dialogue as a verb. "I don't even know how you'd expect to get away with that."

"Here's the thing. I've been working in television a long time, and I know one thing: You two have chemistry."

Zora said, "We had sex, that's not the same thing."

Next to her, Jake cleared his throat.

Felicia brightened again. "You had *great* sex."

The blood rose to her cheeks. "Fine. Whatever. People don't get married because of great sex."

"They have literally been doing that since time began."

Jake spoke, his voice low. "But it would be totally fake, right? That's what you're saying."

"Technically, we'll have to film you getting the license, signing the marriage certificate. We'll have to use a real justice of the peace or watchers will cry foul. So...it'll kind of be real."

Jake drew a finger across his throat. "I never wanted to get married."

Neither had Zora, but it was a shock to hear Jake say it. Everyone else she'd ever known had harbored dreams, even if they were well-hidden, of the Big Day, the day they'd pledge their fidelity to someone forever while wearing really expensive clothes and going into debt for a vacation that was all about sex (that part sounded all right).

It wasn't even that she minded the idea of fidelity. It was sweet, if a little old-fashioned. "Me, neither. The whole idea of marriage is so antiquated."

Jake drew back in what looked like surprise. "Really? That's what I think, too."

"It was a way of brokering chattel. The woman was being impressed into servitude, with no way out. We don't live like that anymore, so why do we still celebrate it?"

Jake nodded enthusiastically. "Exactly. The whole ring thing, the symbol of eternity. Fifty percent of marriages fail. Who looks at those odds and keeps saying that the ring is working?"

Zora said, "People who don't look at reality."

"And what *matters*."

Felicia broke in smoothly, "Just look at you two,

so bonded already. We honestly think this will make for an amazing last episode."

Zora stared. "We literally just broke down why we shouldn't do it."

"So you don't want us to buy your house for you and fix it up."

She wanted that with almost every fiber of her being. "Of course I do. So what, we just get a quickie divorce?"

"Or an annulment. Whatever you prefer we write into the contract."

"I'd get a house. What does he get?"

Jake crossed his arms. "I have a feeling I know."

Felicia nodded. "Enough money to sail away and stay gone for the next two years."

"They're pulling the show," said Jake.

Jolted, Zora said, "Really?"

Jake gestured. "Ask her."

Felicia looked at her lap before raising her gaze and answering. "Jake, you're awesome. You know I literally love you like a brother."

"But the network is tired of me."

"The premise of the show was the Ballard Brothers. Now it's the Jake show, and you've shown no hurry to settle down. That would be good if we were growing the audience, but we haven't been. It's static, and the network needs more. I just got word. This is the last season. But you'll get your wish. You can buy a bigger boat—"

Jake scowled. "Bite your tongue."

"—or go wherever it is you want to go."

"Hmmph."

Yeah, she needed to remember that. Settling down was the last thing Jake Ballard wanted to do. Same with her. She shifted in her seat, moving half an inch farther away from him.

Felicia pressed her hands together. "Here's the deal. You get married. You spend a couple of months living together and getting filmed a couple of times, just for the last few minutes of the epilogue. We can even have the divorce paperwork in the pipes. Then you claim an amicable split, which will be easy since it'll be true. Then, Zora, you have your home sweet home, and Jake, you're living the life of a pirate on the high seas."

"Don't even joke about pirates," Jake muttered.

"What's the problem with any of this? Can either of you think of anything that would prevent us from doing it?"

"Besides morality and the fact that I don't like lying on camera to millions of people?" Zora closed her eyes and thought for a moment. It was crazy. Ludicrous.

But God, she wanted her house, and her garden, and her *gate.* There was another, large part of her that didn't quite think it would be the worst kind of lying ever. She'd never wanted to get married, that was true. But three months with Jake didn't fill her with disgust.

Would it, after all, be the worst thing to wake up next to the guy who'd brought her to orgasm three times in ten minutes last night? She shifted in her seat, and felt a sharp, sweet ache.

The wedding aside, it would be somehow—nice, was that it? Nice to be with him for that time.

And when he sailed away for good, she'd have her house to comfort her. She had an instant image flash into her mind—herself walking the ridgeline of the house, searching the horizon for his boat to sail back into sight.

"I want a widow's walk."

Felicia furrowed her brows. "What's that?"

Jake said, "It's a railed walkway on a roof. Women used to walk and watch for their sailor husbands to come home."

Lord have mercy. Zora hurried to say, "I know, it sounds stupid. I'm *not* going to be watching for you, Ballard. You sail away right off into your bliss. I just think it would add value to the house, and I could get the only full ocean view from the roof anyway. The porch and the yard only give partial views."

His eyes said something that she couldn't quite

understand, but then he turned to Felicia. "I'll do it if she does."

Felicia squared her body to Zora. "And?"

"I'll do it if he does." She felt the tiniest bit queasy at the words.

"Great." Felicia clapped. "Now, we have to work on the proposal. It's gotta be good."

Jake reached sideways and took her hand, his wide palm enveloping Zora's. Her stomach dropped away, and she gripped his fingers. He said, "Whoa. A proposal."

Zora said, "It's going to be the only one I get if I continue to live my life the way I want to. So make it good, huh?" Something occurred to her. "Wait. What if *I* proposed?"

"No, way," Felicia said firmly, "The demographic doesn't want that. The man needs to do that job."

"What kind of sexist crap is that?"

"I don't give a rat's ass about the demographic or sexism, I just know that it *is* my job to do it." Jake tightened his grip on her fingers. "I am so on this. Get ready for the most romantic proposal you've ever seen in your life."

Oh, boy. What was she doing? Was the house worth it?

And why could she barely think about the house? The only thing that was truly registering in

Zora's mind was the feel of her hand in his. Their hands fit each other, just like their bodies had fit together the night before.

God, she was so *confused*. None of this was supposed to happen. Something like fear ran through her—icy and unwelcome. The last time? It hadn't ended so well.

And Jake didn't know the most important thing about her.

"Hey," Jake said. "Look at me."

She did. His deep-water eyes were almost as close to her as they'd been when she came in his arms.

"This will be fun. Nothing more. Just a good time. We're friends, right?"

"Friends," she repeated.

"Let's do this."

Then he kissed her, and even though Zora could faintly hear Felicia say that they were wasting non-filmed heat, she didn't care.

They'd figure it all out later. She kissed him back.

## TWENTY-ONE

Zora's mother wasn't in a good mood. "I don't get it. You stayed last night on Jake Ballard's boat, presumably making it rock, am I right?"

Camille wanted her to be horrified, so while she was, Zora refused to give her that pleasure. "Yes."

Her mother looked pleased. Ridiculously so. "And now you want to stay with your *mother* on a cot in an old-age home. How did you explain that?"

It hadn't been easy. Jake had taken it well, with a small nod. "Of course. Whatever you want." But she'd seen the hurt flash behind his eyes.

Felicia had taken it worse. "But we're paying you to be there."

"That's okay." She was getting a *house*. She didn't need a bonus. And she needed the time—

time to clear her mind and really think about what the hell she was doing. The sex with Jake had been off the charts, and she hadn't even been able to *see* him. It had been better than anything that had ever happened to her body. But her heart was suddenly doing a frantic tango in her chest every time she thought of him. What the hell was she doing?

She needed space. While her body and heart desperately wanted to be on that boat under those covers and under *him*, her brain needed a quiet place to think. He was leaving. Forever. They'd hurt each other in the past so badly. Wasn't this whole thing just set up to be a repeat of that? No hospital involved, of course, unless she needed one for her heart.

She was falling for him again. Last time, it had been fast, too. She'd known on their second date, when he'd taken her on a hike. She'd sprained her ankle leaping a log, and he'd ripped his T-shirt into strips to wrap her ankle and then almost carried her all the way out. This time, though, as a grown-ass woman, it seemed to have happened all at once.

That moment on his boat, they'd almost kissed and hadn't (and then had, again and again and *again*). She'd felt something rise in her, a heat she hadn't been able to name. Yes, it had to do with lust. That was the heat of it. But the loose, helium feeling she felt in her arms and legs every time she thought of him? The way she felt she could almost float away, right up into the sky and then beyond? That feeling was more serious.

How did a person just float back into love? How was that fair? Jake was on the way out of town to accomplish his biggest dream, and she was basically helping him pack. For so long, Zora's focus had been on taking care of herself and her mother—this was the opposite of taking care. This was setting herself up for heartbreak of a kind she could barely imagine.

Zora got milk out of the fridge. She and her mother both loved a salted hot cocoa at night, but it had to be real, heated on the stove. "Is there a problem with wanting to stay with my mother?"

"For a night or maybe two, if no one turns you in for using our water in the shower? No, except that you could be getting some hot sailor action and you're choosing not to, so yeah, that part of it is wrong."

"Please don't say that again."

"What?" Camille's eyes brightened. "Hot sailor action? Honey, you should hear what goes on around here. Last week, Felicity and Grover got caught banging in the broom closet, but Grover slipped on a Swiffer and broke his hip. Felicity was back in the same broom closet with Nicholas three days later. She says the smell of bleach gets her horny."

Another word she never needed to hear from her mother, ever again. "I'm just a little confused about him, that's all."

"What is there to be confused *about*? He's gorgeous. He's a TV star. When he goes to San Francisco, I bet ladies throw their panties at him."

"It's cold there. I don't think they'd take the time to strip off their leggings." Zora stirred the milk, the gas on the highest setting. The quicker she and her mother drank the hot cocoa, the quicker her mother would insist on getting into bed and turning off all the lights. Then Zora could stare into the darkness and let herself feel it again—the way he'd kissed her last night, into a raging inferno of desire that she matched, coming back again and again for more.

"They want us to get married for the show," she said, pulling down the chocolate and the marshmallows.

Her mother went into a coughing fit. Her remote-controlled chair sent her up and then down again, as if she couldn't decide what to do with it. "Excuse me?"

"Just a stunt. But it means I get to buy my cottage. The one I live in."

Camille pressed a hand to her chest. "Oh, *honey.*"

"I know, right?"

"You'd have a real *home.*"

Zora nodded.

"For the first time ever."

"Not true." Zora added chocolate, vanilla, and sugar to the almost-boiling milk and stirred it. "I always had a home. I just didn't know you didn't have one."

Her mother concentrated on fiddling with the chair controller and didn't respond.

"So you don't think it's crazy?"

Camille jerked up her head. "Oh, yeah. It's nutballs."

"We'll be able to get divorced a few months later when the press heat is off."

"Well, that just sucks."

"But you got divorced."

"I don't mean that. I mean that in order to win your ultimate freedom, you have to tie yourself, however briefly, to the man who hurt you."

The milk started boiling over, and Zora barely noticed. "I know."

Camille pointed at the pot. "Turn that off. You're making a mess, and I don't want to clean it up."

"You have housekeeping."

"But I'm not rude to them. Clean it when it cools."

"Yes, ma'am," Zora said automatically. She carefully poured the mixture into two cups and added exactly ten mini-marshmallows to each. "Do you think he'll hurt me again?"

"Well, it's impossible to hurt you the same way, right?"

She handed a mug to her mother. "It's just for the house. Just for the show." *But I'm scared.*

"You've always loved him."

"Mother. I have not."

Camille nodded. "Try it. Say you weren't in love with him in high school."

"I was *not* in love with Jake Ballard in high school. We were in very strong like."

Camille reached for the small hand mirror on her side table and held it up. "The tip of your nose goes red when you lie."

"Are you calling me Rudolph?" Zora looked. Yep. Her nose was red. "I must have gotten some sun."

"You were in love with him, he knocked you up, and you never really got over him."

Zora felt herself flinch. It hadn't been getting knocked up. It had been getting sick, then sicker, and then so sick she was in the hospital for two weeks. The ectopic pregnancy almost killed her.

Her mother had told everyone, including Jake when he'd tried to visit her, that she'd had a gall-bladder infection. When the doctor told Zora that they'd had to do an emergency hysterectomy, she'd felt nothing but numbness, as if the anesthesia had flooded her whole body. Numb brain, numb heart.

When her mother had finally allowed Jake in to see her, she'd simply said, "I'll see you when I get out of here."

"I just want to sit with you for a while."

"We'll meet at the beach when I'm better."

Jake had just gone white as the muscle in his jaw jumped. Had he known then what she was going to do? "You sure?"

"Yes."

"And are you really okay?"

Zora had lost the ability to speak by then. She nodded.

He'd stood, giving her one last look that she couldn't interpret. Did he believe her?

Then he'd left.

Now, hot chocolate in hand, Zora said, "It was just bad luck and bad timing."

Camille slurped a marshmallow. "Lie all you want, but you were in crazy love with the kid, and you're back in it now."

"Mom." Her voice was twisted in her throat.

"Can we *not* do this? I've got to marry the guy. I need to keep the feelings to a dull roar."

"Does he know you're infertile?"

Zora's head throbbed. She stood and poured out the second half of her cocoa. "I'm going to bed."

"Wait! You have to tell me about the shoot and what he's like now and who those camera people know. Do they know Connie Britton, you think? Because I have something to tell her about what she should do with her hair. She's getting too old to wear it so long, although God knows it's pretty like that."

Zora dropped a kiss on the thin white hair at the top of her mother's head. "Goodnight, Ma. Thanks for letting me stay." They'd put the cot in the half-sized office.

"You can't stay more than a couple of nights. Water restriction, you know. Evelyn in 119 will turn me in."

"I thought you were best friends."

"She cheats at bridge." The worst thing a person could do, in Camille's eyes. She'd rather chat with a murderer than a person who cheated at cards.

"Love you, Mom."

"Did you throw out the rest of your cocoa? That was dumb. Why didn't you give it to me?" Camille rode her chair up and down a few times and then tottered to her bedroom. At the doorway, she turned. "I'm sorry, honey. I just don't know what to say to you sometimes."

It was the best her mother could do, she knew that. Zora got in bed, the cold rigidity the very opposite of the super-heated bed she'd been in the night before. She tried very hard not to think about herself in a white dress. Whenever she failed, she immediately thought of Jake in a tux, a thought that made her lose her breath.

Her phone pinged. *I can't stop thinking about you.*

Carefully, she turned off the ringer. She slid the phone under her pillow. She wouldn't respond yet —she was too confused. But knowing his message had landed there, in her phone, just under her head, was comforting. Hopefully, it would ease the longing she felt in her heart.

# TWENTY-TWO

Jake slept worse than he had in years. He dreamed that Zora was on the boat, but he couldn't find her. He dreamed that they were at sea and that she'd fallen overboard in a storm. Twice he woke thinking there was something evil in his bed, something that had taken Zora, but it turned out both times to be the pillow wadded up under his back.

She'd said she needed to be with her mom. She needed time to think. And Jake totally got it. While he was fixing coffee for himself, he knew that the fact that she was taking care of herself was a good thing.

He just wished he were making coffee for two.

When he got to Zora's house, Aidan and Zora were already filming in the kitchen. Felicia gave him the *stop making noise* look as he tried to sneak his way in.

God, Zora looked so pretty. Dressed in a loose, yellow V-necked shirt and a pair of fitted jeans, she looked classy and casual at the same time. Yeah, she kind of looked like a fourth-grade teacher. And yeah, that turned him on.

Zora said to Aidan, "I want to keep all the appliances."

"No, way. We've got to get you up to code, at least. The exhaust fan above your range isn't even linked to a vent, you know that? Every time you've ever used that fan, you've just been blowing it all back into the kitchen."

"Well," said Zora. "That explains a lot, actually. Can you install a vent?"

"Sure, but—"

"I love my stove." She ran her hands over the white enamel. "It stays."

"Not the fridge, though, right?" Aidan's face looked strained. "It's yellow."

"I love it. Can you have someone refurbish it? Like, look at the guts and make sure it's going to work for a while longer?"

A camera zoomed in front of Jake, blocking his view for a moment. He craned his neck to continue watching her.

Aidan plastered on his woman-pleasing smile,

the one that had won him the love of his life on an early show. "What about a nice KitchenAid fridge? You wouldn't have to do anything to it or for it for the next ten years, maybe fifteen. This old one has maybe another week or two. I think it's been here since the sixties anyway."

Zora wobbled. "Stainless steel?"

"You bet."

"I hate stainless steel."

Aidan took a breath. Jake's brother was a big sweetie, but he wasn't the best with customer relations. Those usually fell to Liam, or in a pinch, Jake himself. "What about a yellow fridge, same color, but state of the art innards. Two different ice options. Bluetooth."

Zora said, "Now you're kidding me."

"Nope." Aidan definitely wasn't using his kidding voice.

"Okay, then. Yes." She looked toward Jake and seemed surprised to see him standing there. Did she not want him on set? He couldn't read her face—was that pleasure to see him? Or alarm? What was going on, and how could Jake fix it?

She pulled off her mic. "Can we take a break?"

Felicia logged something on her ever-present iPad. "Sure. Everyone take five. Hey, Jake. I have to talk to you and Zora."

*He* needed to talk to Zora. But it could wait, he supposed. It would have to.

She hadn't met his eyes yet.

"Where's quiet around here?" Felicia looked to her right and left. "Where in this falling down house is there a place we can have some peace?"

"My bedroom?" Zora pointed.

"Great."

As they followed Felicia through Zora's house, Jake said in a low voice, "How are you?"

"I'm good." She said it cheerfully. What did that actually mean? Was she good? Had she slept well, without a thought of him?

Her room wasn't quite what he'd expected. Somehow, he'd pictured a fourth-grade teacher's bedroom, all light colors and pastels and very tidy. Instead, she had red walls and bright yellow dahlia prints. The curtains were light gray and floor-length. Her bed was simple, with a wooden headboard. There was a pile of clothes on the floor next to the closet, shoes tossed in all directions, and her bed was unmade.

It felt like her, sexy and vivid and luscious. It smelled like her, lemon and sugar.

Zora perched on the bed and pulled her feet up under her. "It always looks this messy—this isn't the car's fault."

"Okay," said Felicia, bouncing a little on her

feet. "Good news. We're going to get most of this done in the next two weeks. The show wants to move up production and release. Another show crashed and burned, and they want us to fill the slot with this season. We've got three other construction companies coming in to assist with the rebuild. Zora, I have a ton of paperwork for you to sign off on."

Zora nodded.

"How can I help?" Jake wanted to get into the job and get his hands dirty. Rip down some old walls, put up new ones. His favorite thing was hanging drywall, which made him popular on whatever crew he was on. He wanted to put this coiled tension in his body toward something useful.

"Yeah. I need you to pull some strings."

"Done. Consider me your string-puller."

Zora gave a soft snort.

Felicia, though, gave him a nod of appreciation. "Great. I need you to call a surf instructor. Can we get you out there this afternoon?"

Jake blinked. "I know how to surf."

"Not for you, for her." Felicia pointed at Zora.

Zora held up one hand. "I've managed to live in this town most of my life and haven't taken up surfing yet. I have to do it now?"

"Not for long. Just long enough for us to get some establishing shots. It's a great date idea that we've never done on the show. Jake, can you handle that?"

"I mean, I can ask a buddy to meet us out there with some rental gear for her, but it depends on the waves."

"See what you can do. Hopefully, we can do it this afternoon. Then tomorrow, you drive to Napa together and go wine tasting at a place I know. We'll just take a few short shots with you two sipping wine, then we can get you back out here to do something inside the house together—hammering nails or slopping paint on a wall. Sound good?"

Jake felt his head spin—hell, yes, these were things he wanted to do with Zora. Teach her to surf? He wanted to do that and then watch her sit on her board in a wetsuit, watch the way the light played on her face, watch her hair tangle in wet clumps that would look sexy as hell on her. Take her to Napa and drink wine and then dine by a fire? He couldn't think of anything (that happened clothed) that he wanted to do more with her.

Felicia continued, "We can start working on B-roll and planning the proposal and the wedding at the same time. Should be able to wind up the house reno and the wedding quickly, getting this on the air in less than a month."

A month? With the reno done in two weeks? That had to be next to impossible, and he could tell by the look on Felicia's face that she didn't believe her own words.

But they could try, right? And it would be fun to do exactly that.

He'd try just about anything with Zora. He spent a moment wishing that they were alone in this room. That he could mess up her bed even more with her.

Zora nodded. "The faster, the better."

The words could have meant that she was eager to be with him, but her voice made it sound like she just wanted to get it over with. It stung a bit. "You in a hurry?"

She busied herself fluffing a pillow. "Hey, you're the one who's going to sail away."

Funny. That dream seemed less important than it ever had. What would it be like to just stay?

Staying with Zora.

Jake's mouth went dry. *This* was why he didn't date seriously. He couldn't be tied down. He was a wanderer. His roots were so shallow they didn't even go into the dirt, just into his boat's deck. He edged himself closer to the door, making Tony dart into the far corner with his camera.

Felicia said, "The network wants this, so they'll throw money at it. In my experience, money makes everything go as fast as we need it to. The only thing we've got to worry about is beefing up your romance storyline so that the world believes you actually want to get married practically overnight."

Funny. That was the one thing Jake wasn't worried about. "Oh, that won't be hard."

Zora looked at him, and the rest of the room dropped away. There was no one there, no camera on him, no brother or producer around. "You don't think so?"

"I'd run away with you to Vegas right now."

"Cameras on us all the way?"

"I wouldn't need a single camera."

Her eyes softened, and something shifted between them—he could feel it. Zora was easier in her skin, and a smile tugged at her lips. She said, "No wedding selfies?"

"Okay, one picture taken on a cell phone. A selfie, right after we say *I do*. Just for us."

"Just for us." Her voice was quiet.

"Let them take all the fancy posed pictures they want. I'd just want that one that we took. That's the photo that would matter. That would tell me we'd actually done it. We'd blow it up and put it over the fireplace in a fancy frame."

Zora's gaze didn't waver. "It's a good thing we don't have time to get to Vegas, then. We'd ruin the whole show."

"Yeah." His voice came out hoarse. Her gaze, smoldering and heated, was still locked on him. Jesus, if he could get her into a room where they wouldn't get interrupted...

Felicia stepped between them. "Right! Before we have to hit you both with the water hose, get yourself and Zora into those waves, okay? Tell me where to send the crew. Hey!" She spun. "Who on the crew surfs? We need a camera on these two at all times!"

Not at *all* times. He'd manage to get her away from the cameras as soon as was humanly possible. Or sooner.

# TWENTY-THREE

It turned out that zipping oneself into a wetsuit wasn't as easy as it looked on TV. Zora grunted as she dragged the zipper pull upward. Jake had just slipped out of his jeans right there in the parking lot, displaying his lobster boxers, so adorable Zora felt the desire to grab him by the elastic of them and pull him toward her—she only just prevented herself. He'd stepped into his wetsuit, and his zipper had slipped up with seeming ease, enclosing him in a black bodysuit and sadly hiding the ripped torso that made her yearn to touch him. On the plus side, the wetsuit made him look like a freaking superhero.

Her, though? Not the same experience. She'd

stripped to her bathing suit, regretting her choice of the bikini as soon as she'd lifted her shirt. She could feel their eyes—his and the camera crews'—on her round belly that pooched out softly. It matched her thighs, which rubbed, and the fat roll at her back where her top was tied.

But she'd already stepped into the wetsuit, so she had to go forward with it. "I'm going to need a bigger one, I think." Better to say it herself and pretend that she was clinging to some dignity than to have a staffer yell it out for her. God, what was this? She had healthy self-esteem. Her body, though not small, was strong. Made for hard work. Made for hard play. She *liked* her soft body. But she sure as hell wasn't enjoying knowing it would be judged by America in a couple of weeks.

She wanted to wrap herself in the nearest blanket (she could see one in the back of his truck, just lying there, all warm and unused) and get out of there.

"It's fine. It'll stretch," said Jake.

She wiggled it up over her hips, just barely. "Oh, God."

"Arms in next, don't zip it until you've done that."

Tony and Anna were looking at a screen and not paying any attention to them, thank God. Only

Jake was watching her, and that was more than enough.

"Do you want help?"

"I do *not* want help." She gave a hop and tugged on the thick rubber. Damn it, she just wasn't strong enough to pull it up any farther, and if she didn't, she wouldn't be able to get her arms in. She sighed. "Fine. Help."

"Yep. No problem." That was his all-business voice, but it didn't help her in the slightest to remain calm when he was so close to her that she could smell the rubber of his suit and something sweeter and darker, like cocoa or rum.

He slid his hands up her hips, underneath the folded rubber, and grasped both sides of the suit. He pulled right and then left.

Zora's breasts brushed his suit. Hopefully it was thick enough that he hadn't felt that in detail like she just had. His eyes, though, said that even if he hadn't felt how hard her nipples were, he could see them under the thin material of her bikini.

He cleared his throat and gave one more tug. "Okay. Try again."

Her arms went into the suit, and, with relief, she was able to pull up the zipper that ran from her waist to her neck. Instantly, she was covered and grateful. "Damn, this is like Spanx." She patted her tummy, her friend again now that it wasn't exposed to ocean air. "I've got a little black dress I should wear this under."

"Please don't."

"I was just kidding—"

"You're the most beautiful girl in the world. Exactly the way you are."

The words should have sounded like a cliché, but coming from Jake's mouth, they sounded like they'd never been said before in the history of flirtation. Lord have mercy, they were going to have to call her an ambulance if her heart rate sped up any more. Jake had *always* been able to get to her. Nothing ever changed, did it? What could she say to that?

There was really one thing. "Thank you."

"You're welcome." Jake reached forward and tugged the zip up the last fraction of an inch. Even with the wetsuits between them, she could feel his heat. If she tilted her head up just a little...

He put one hand behind the nape of her neck. Leaning down, he whispered in her ear, "You're incredible." He dropped a swift kiss on her gasping mouth before pulling away. He repeated, "Always."

A second later, after she'd caught her breath, she planted her hands on her rubber-clad hips. "Jake. Is this a good idea?"

"Which part? The surfing? The show? The wedding?"

She spread her hands. "All of it."

"Oh, yeah. It's a good idea."

"Which part?"

He grinned, and something slow and sweet like honey moved in her belly. "*All* of it," he said.

# TWENTY-FOUR

Jake's friend Riggs gave Zora a good board for her size, but Jake wanted to teach her the moves himself. It was just an excuse to be as near to her as possible, and it was a good one. On the sand, he showed her how to pop up, drop, trim, and turn.

*All of it,* he'd said. Even marriage. He'd never, *ever* wanted to be married, but now? Sliding a ring onto Zora's finger sounded like the most natural and wonderful thing on earth. Not for the piece of paper—he could give a rat's ass about that. It was her. In spite of the circus that was the show, he wanted *her* by his side, and he wanted to be by hers. His gut had always told him to steer clear of contracts about love, but now his gut was certain—he would sign a contract to her in blood if she wanted him to.

What was *happening* to him? Jake didn't know. More—he didn't care. He was here now, teaching her to surf, and that was all he needed in this moment. Zora was strong and sure, and she took his instruction with a laugh and what looked like eagerness.

In the water, though, she changed.

Paddling out was okay. Her upper arms were strong, and she seemed to keep up with him easily.

But when they were sitting on their boards, she was tight, her face closed. Her body was tensed with none of her usual ease.

"Hey, you okay?"

She smiled thinly and glanced at Tony who floated on his board thirty feet away, his camera in its waterproof case pointed at them. They wore waterproof mics, but he'd promised to stay far enough away so that they could safely try to catch a wave when one came by.

"Fine," she said.

She didn't look fine. "What is it?"

"Are there sharks out here?"

Jake wished he could tell her no, but he wouldn't lie to her. "There might be a few, but they're not interested in us."

"Can they smell fear?"

"What are you scared of?"

"Dying in the ocean by being eaten by sharks."

"Really?"

She shot an annoyed glance at him. "Yes, really. Why do you think I've never surfed after growing up in a beach town?"

"Wow," he said. "You're afraid of the ocean, and you didn't say a thing."

"Why bother?"

"Most people do."

"I knew it was an unreasonable fear."

"Yeah?"

"Yeah. I know there are sharks. And I know they leave people alone." A swell underneath them made her bob first, then him. She looked so *natural* on the board, like she'd been there her whole life. Her hair was still dry—he longed to see it wet and matted together in ocean-made clumps.

"Why'd you ask then?"

"You know how when the milk is going bad, you ask someone else to smell it?"

"Uh-huh."

"It's like that. I needed to hear you say that they weren't interested in us."

"Even though you already knew it."

She nodded.

"I get that."

Zora gave a short laugh. "No, you don't."

"What do you mean I don't?"

"You're a guy. Guys don't need reassurance. They don't need to come to a consensus before making decisions. You just feel something and then do it."

"That's sexist and mostly wrong." He didn't feel offended, though.

Zora looked at the beach. "Probably. Are we drifting?"

Short gusts of wind were blowing them slowly southward, but the opposite current was keeping them mostly in place. They'd be fine where they were a little longer. "We're okay. You want to know what's under us?"

He could actually see her gulp.

But she said, "Yeah. Please."

"Okay. Close your eyes." He got close enough to her that he could catch the edge of her board. "I've got you. No fear."

She shut her eyes tightly, her hands in fists on her thighs.

He kept his voice low, just loud enough for her to catch. "You're safe on your surfboard. The water wants to hold you up, and it's not going to stop wanting that. You're floating in just the right way. Underneath is more water, also interested in holding you safely on the surface. There's a layer of soft sand about fifteen feet below us. As the tides come in and out, as the waves move, the sand shifts, rolling on top of itself. If you hold your ears just under the water, you can hear the sand crunching against itself. There are some big rocks down there, too, and some fish dart around them. You might see your largemouth bass, some flounder, a bluegill, or a steelhead. Not very many, though. Most of the space underneath you is empty. Just like a bathtub but with salt water. And on top of all of this ocean, we're sitting next to each other." Without thinking, he caught her hand. Her fingers were cold, and she clutched his hand tightly. They bobbed separately, then together, as another small swell moved underneath them. He could feel a good wave building behind them.

"And now it's time to open your eyes. I'm going to let you go. When the swell builds, you're going to paddle forward, just like we practiced on the sand. Then you're going to pop up when you feel like the wave is about to break, okay?"

Her eyes were huge, locked on to his. "What if I fall?"

"Oh, you'll fall, all right. You just get up again, that's all. You try it again."

The wave built behind them and started to break at just the right point. "Now!" he called. "Pop up!"

He only caught half of it himself before falling

out. When he surfaced and cleared his eyes, he couldn't find her for a second. Jesus. What if he was wrong? What if she was, actually, being carried out by a riptide, or caught underwater by her hair on a rock, or what if the practically-impossible had happened and she *was* getting eaten by a shark—

Then he saw her, almost to shore, much farther away than he would have predicted. Still standing, her arms windmilling, but *surfing*.

Laughing all the way.

## TWENTY-FIVE

It was glorious. Being with *him* out on the water was, bar none, one of the best feelings Zora had ever felt in her entire life. Jake told her she was a natural, and she believed it. He insisted she must have done it when she was a kid but, for one, Camille would never have allowed that, and for two, Zora would have remembered.

But it did feel *good.*

Being on the water, waiting for the wave, was almost the best part. Sure, riding a wave into shore was exhilarating. It felt good in her body, in her bones. She finally understood how people turned their whole lives inside out to chase the waves.

But really, sitting on her board close to Jake, that was the best part. Sometimes they drifted far apart, but when they caught each other's eyes, there was something deep and sweet and *hot* underneath their gaze. Other times they were so close that even with the constant *shushhh*ing of the waves, they didn't have to speak loudly to be heard.

Jake was so...oh, damn, he was everything.

"I remember this feeling," she said, unable to keep the words in her mouth. She wasn't talking about being in the water, and she didn't care that they wore mics—whatever they said related to the past would probably be nonsensical to someone who didn't know their history. But this feeling—it had to be acknowledged. The feeling of being *known*. Being seen. He'd always looked at her in a way that no one else ever had—like she was something special and wonderful. His gaze stayed soft, his features open, readable. He was doing it now every time she looked at him, which was every few seconds. Gazing at him felt like a hit of a really good drug, and she couldn't stop doing it.

He looked thrilled, as if she was doing something amazing just by sitting on a surfboard.

Like she was beautiful. He'd said it. His face made her believe he meant it.

He just looked at her. Then he nodded.

She used her legs to swing her board so that she was facing him. "You know what I mean?"

He nodded again. "I do."

Oh, God. *I do.* The words they would say to each other on camera.

She pushed back her salt-tangled wet hair. On another day, she would have felt like a mess. No makeup, hair a rat's nest—but not with the way he was looking at her. "I love it out here."

"I can tell. What do you love best?"

"Being here with you."

He glowed. "What else?"

"The feeling when you catch the wave. Like you're almost out of control, and you're falling, and then you're just *in* it for what feels like forever but I know is probably only seconds." So similar to the way she felt when their gazes tangled.

Jake gave her a smile so full of sexiness and sweetness that no amount of money would have been able to convince Zora to take her eyes off him. The network could offer her another house, and she'd turn it down. She just wanted to keep looking at him, with this lightweight, helium-like feeling in her chest, as if she were about to float into the sky.

He paddled closer and then slid off his board. "Come here. Maybe they can't hear us if we whisper."

She didn't even pause to think. She slipped off her own surfboard.

He kept one hand on his surfboard for buoyancy, and she did the same, but their wetsuited bodies pressed against each other.

Jake's arm wrapped around her back, as her free arm twined around his neck. The kiss was fast and wet, his lips cold against hers, heating up almost instantly. His tongue was salty and sweet, making her hunger for so much more than kisses in the water.

This man. *This* one.

They pulled apart. Zora couldn't help laughing into the sky out of what felt like pure joy.

Then Jake said, "Marry me."

Zora blinked. "Aren't you supposed to do that on camera? Like a whole proposal thing?"

"Yeah, I'll do that. I can't wait to do that. But I wanted one as off the record as we can get, too." He popped up and looked over his board. Tony was still on the far side, probably trying to zoom in as much as he could. But between their boards, with only their heads out of the water, the space felt intimate. Private. "I'm going to ask you again, you ready for it?"

Bubbles of delight swam through her blood. "Yes."

"Zora, will you marry me?"

A swell raised them and dropped them. Their fingers interlaced.

Zora took a deep breath. "Yes."

Jake gave a whoop of delight and drew her in

for another kiss. Zora lost her breath and her brain, and by the time Tony had paddled close enough to train his camera on them, she'd almost forgotten how to tread water.

"Whatever you guys just did, can you do it again?" called Tony, struggling with his Steadicam. "I didn't even get it on audio."

Jake snorted. "Wasn't for you, my friend. It was just for her."

A wavelet slapped Zora in the face, sending water up her nose. Her ankle-strap tugged. Jake pulled away, giving her that heated look again, and then got up on his board. "Want to take another ride, Zora?"

Oh, yeah. She did.

And at the same time, she was terrified. Why had he asked her like that, in private? What did that mean? Like he'd really meant it? When she'd said yes, she had meant that with all her heart.

And that was completely terrifying. Being on camera, on the show, falling for her old flame—that was one thing.

Did they both really mean it? And how could she be sure? If they did mean it, how would it actually go, being in love with a man who didn't even want to stay on the continent?

She pulled herself up onto her board, barking her shin as she did so.

Suddenly, she didn't want to try to stand up when the next good set came in. It felt way too dangerous. What was she *doing* out here? There could be ten sharks circling under her right now, getting ready to divide her body from her legs.

But why would she need legs, if she had already lost her heart?

It was gone, she realized.

She'd lost it to Jake for the second time in her life. Last time hadn't ended up so well. This time, it was almost all on film, and no matter what was in Jake's gaze, it was probably all pretend—they'd established that already.

What could possibly go wrong with a plan like that?

For a terrible moment, Zora wished to feel the razor-pain of shark teeth locking around her leg. It would probably hurt less than what lay ahead.

# TWENTY-SIX

Jake saw Zora dart down the hallway toward the kitchen, a coil of steel strapping over her arm. He lifted his hand and grinned, but she didn't see him, her eyes on the ground as she moved fast.

It was the third time, actually, that she hadn't noticed him when he'd been trying to catch her eye. He'd told himself the first two times that she was busy.

Now, though.

She was avoiding him. His gaze. Shit.

"Jesus, Jake! Do you ever look at what you're doing?" Aidan caught Jake's arm right as he was about to swing his paintbrush right over the blue painter's tape as if it wasn't even there.

"Sorry."

Aidan said, "Dude. Wake up. Go get some coffee if you need it. Are you hungover or something?"

Hungover? No. Drunk? A little bit, but not on alcohol. He was drunk on the thought of Zora. She'd still been spending nights with her mother, which was probably good because if she *had* stayed on the boat, they'd have gotten no sleep at all, and Jake would be painting the floor and his shoes along with the walls.

All hands were on deck today, and Zora was in the kitchen helping install the plumbing for the new washer. He could hear her laughing with Felicia sometimes, and each time he heard it, the front of his brain lit with pleasure and he forgot how to hold a paintbrush.

She'd said *yes*.

Of course, Jake had known that she probably would. That was the whole plan, after all, but the fact that he'd asked her off-camera made it real to him. And hopefully to her.

He'd *wanted* the proposal to be real. That was the terrifying and best part of it all. When he'd asked her in the water, he'd seen a whole montage of images. Her in a small chapel, wearing white, walking toward him. No one else was there. He hadn't even seen a minister. Just the two of them.

Her, on his boat, her hair pulled up in a handkerchief as she trimmed the mainsail. Him, in her backyard, starting up the barbecue while she sat on the bench with a book and a cat in her lap and laughed in his direction. He imagined digging holes for her to plant more trees.

For the first time in years, he had a reason to want to stay in Darling Bay.

He couldn't, of course. He was going to have enough money to get out of town and stay out of town—out of the country—for years. Exactly what he wanted the most. Alone, just like he'd planned it.

And alone was exactly what he was going to get, too, since no matter what his heart kept telling him, no matter how her eyes lit when she looked at him, Zora had been avoiding the hell out of him since their surfing afternoon.

She was still being nice. She'd smiled at him when he'd arrived, and it had looked real. Heat had flared between them, just like the electricity that snapped between them whenever they had to touch. She'd passed him a hammer the day before, and she'd let her fingers linger in his. They'd had one seriously shoe-melting make-out session behind the rose arbor two days before. Jake had never been so happy and confused as after she'd said yes to him, to the proposal that felt like it meant much more than a fake, scripted one, and he'd thought she'd felt the same way: confused, scared, elated, blissful.

But actually *talking?* Zora hadn't given him a single chance to ask about a thing since they left the water. She'd been running scared. When he got close enough to ask her anything, she stopped him with a kiss, and boy howdy, was she good at stopping him from holding onto conscious thought.

One night after a late evening of plaster-pulling, he'd asked, "Hey, Zora, you want to get dinner with me tonight?"

Felicia had yelled, "Tony and Anna have the night off! No dinner for you!"

Jake had said, "Just the two of us. No cameras. We deserve a break."

But Zora had just shaken her head and said, "Gotta check on my mom tonight."

She was *staying* with her mom, so seeing her didn't seem like a totally credible excuse. He wanted desperately to ask her to stay on the boat again with him, but he was pretty sure he'd get shot down. Usually, Jake didn't mind rejection. If a woman said no to him, she had a reason, and he didn't have to know what it was.

He just didn't think he could take getting shot down by Zora.

The trip to Napa had been excruciating enough. It had been a glorious day, with golden sun and a cool breeze. The wine had been crisp, the limousine smooth. Zora had said all the right things for the camera. She'd smiled and flirted mildly and leaned against him when the moon rose over the vines.

The crew had captured the best footage they'd gotten so far, they said. Felicia had seemed ecstatic.

And the whole thing had rung hollow to Jake. Even when they'd sat in the middle of the grapevines at a small table lit with tiny white lights, even when he'd poured champagne into her crystal flute, even when he'd held her hand and kissed the tips of each of her fingers, there was something missing.

That something was Zora herself.

He'd come up with the idea of having his high school letter jacket in a basket nearby, and when it had gotten cold in the vineyard, he'd draped the same jacket over her shoulders that he had when they were teenagers. The ring he'd offered her was two carats, and she'd get to keep it afterward no matter what happened—he'd made sure Felicia got that approved from the network.

She'd smiled and said yes. She'd looked amazing, as always, the jacket over her shoulders taking him right back to what she'd looked like at eighteen. Her deep brown eyes so huge, the lashes fringing them seeming almost miraculous. It was true—she was hotter now than she'd ever been. But even more than that, she was prettier, too.

But Jake had pulled her against him, his arms felt almost empty. Only her kiss felt like her—she couldn't stop the heat that flared between them, the electricity that sparked their skin every time they touched. When he was kissing her, they were truly together—he could tell. But as soon as she pulled back, she wasn't just a foot away. She was a million miles gone.

And he had no idea what he'd done.

"Jake!" Aidan's shout was right next to Jake's head.

"Shit." Jake had painted over the tape and onto the doorjamb. "I'll cover it up."

"You bet your ass you will. I'd give you an easier job, but I honestly can't think of one. What is *wrong* with you?"

Jake dropped the brush into the paint pan. "Look. Can we talk?"

Aidan crossed his arms. "Shoot."

Here? Couldn't they go out on the porch or something farther away from the room Zora was in? But Aidan looked immovable. Jake didn't feel like getting into a physical tussle, and there were no cameras in here at the moment, so he guessed it would do.

"Something's changed with Zora and me."

He could tell Aidan barely restrained himself from rolling his eyes. "You're on camera all the time.

That does it."

"It's bigger than that."

"Oh, yeah. You're both not into getting married. You just have to get through the wedding and then a couple months later, you'll be on your own again, and you can finally go on your trip. Hang in there."

"But I don't want to be on my own." Only when the words came out of his mouth did he realize how true they were. "Oh, damn it. I *don't* want to be on my own."

Aidan laughed. The bastard.

"Aidan."

That made his brother laugh harder. "Oh, my God. This is so great."

"This is not great."

Aidan bent at the waist, resting his hands on his tool belt, and took several deep breaths. "*Whoo.* Stop. You're killing me." He wiped his eyes. "This is too good. You got caught on dry land. I *knew* it."

"This is the worst." Even as he said it, Jake knew he was wrong. It was the best. Being in love with Zora wasn't something he wanted to turn off.

Or did he?

"How can you tell if it's a good thing or a bad thing?"

Aidan straightened both his body and his face. "Okay. Real talk?"

Jake stuck his hands in his pockets and braced

himself. If he and his brothers talked about emotions at all, they did it over beers. Not in the bright light of day at *work*. And usually, he bared his soul more to Liam, who'd always had a longer fuse, who was more likely to cheer him on than tell him to buck up and get over it. But he needed advice, and he needed it now. "Yeah."

"If you're in love with her, really in love, don't wait."

"Wait? This show is literally the opposite of waiting. We're getting *married*." The words still didn't feel real in his mouth.

"You know what I mean. All that's fake. Don't wait to show her how you feel."

He'd proposed in the ocean. A real proposal, one that he'd barely seen coming. One that he'd meant with his heart, utterly. "What if she doesn't feel the same way?"

"Then at least you weren't the one who blew the chance of a lifetime, right?"

"What do you mean?"

Aidan fiddled with the measuring tape strapped to his waist, pulling out the tape and letting it snap back. "You think she's the one?"

Jake felt a punch to his solar plexus. "Yeah. I do."

"You can't change her feelings, whatever they

are. But you can show her yours. If you don't, you risk losing her entirely."

They were big words coming from his quiet brother. "I hear you."

"Dude, if I didn't have Tuesday, I wouldn't have a life worth living."

"Come on. You were fine before her."

"I *was* fine. I feel like I was living in black and white. Everything was okay." Aidan gave a short laugh and rubbed the top of his head. "Now it's all color. How do you go from color back to black and white?"

"You don't."

Aidan turned to face the street. "You can't."

"So you stay on dry land." The words weren't as hard to say as he thought they'd be.

"Sure. Or you find a place between the ocean and the land where you both can live."

Jake squinted at his brother. "Like a swamp."

"Whatever. You know what I mean."

Jake nodded. He did.

TWENTY-SEVEN

As Zora sanded a new cutting board in the student garden, the air smelled of sawdust and the dusty sycamore leaves overhead. She sat in one of the wobbly Adirondacks a student's parent had made. From her seat, she could look into her own garden. The grapes she'd planted the year before looked happy on the arbor. She'd gotten a few small bunches this year, and next year there would be even more. And she would get to stay and harvest them.

She'd always known that someday she'd have to leave the garden behind—it was a rental, after all. But she'd let herself get attached. Now she didn't have to let go.

Jake, though. He was in the picture. And what a

picture it was.... The image of his naked torso as he'd pulled on his wetsuit, the way his eyes would lock with hers and not let go as her stomach flipped in happy butterfly circles....

He was also temporary, she reminded herself as she sanded carefully and quickly with long, deliberate strokes. This was all a ruse, after all, and she *had* to start remembering that. They were pulling the wool over the eyes of viewers, treating them to a "real" love affair when in reality, they were doing it for the money. She, to get a house. He, to leave forever on his boat.

What the hell had that been in the ocean, then?

It had felt as though he'd been asking with his heart. As though he actually *wanted* to marry her. For real.

The astonishing thing was that she'd said yes. She'd said it with her heart.

Marriage. Bah. She hadn't even wanted to date much for the past two years. Jake had come back into her life for a minute, and she could suddenly see a *wedding*, a real one?

She was losing her goddamned mind along with her heart. Come to think of it, she should be nothing but glad it wasn't going to be a real wedding.

If it wasn't real, she'd never have to tell him

about her infertility, her secret from everyone but her mother.

That's why it couldn't be real. Zora *couldn't* want this, or want him.

She could never tell him the truth she'd hidden so long.

"Miss Zora! Miss Zora!" Petra Nuñes and her little sister Vera ran toward her. "We saw you here, and Daddy's going to the hardware store! Can we help you while he's there? Are you gardening?"

Their father, Juan Nuñes, leaned out of his truck and waved. "Just say the word and I'll put them back in the car, Zora."

"No, that's fine," she called. "I've got some weeding that I really need help with."

Every year, there were two or three kids who didn't forget the garden over the summer. They'd show up at random times and knock at her door, asking her to unlock the tool shed, to water with them. She'd send them home with bags full of produce. This year, those kids were Petra and Vera.

She turned to them, hands on her hips. "Wow. I'm so glad you're here. Let's start weeding around the tomato plants, okay? Remember how we talked about the big fuzzy stalk of the tomato? Let's pull up everything around it that isn't part of the main plant."

For fifteen minutes, Zora forgot about the

house, about the sanding, about almost everything else. Petra had been one of her favorite students the year before. Always inquisitive and deeply kind, the girl was going to go far, she could just feel it. She *did* have favorites. She loved all her kids, but some got into her soul, and Petra had been one of them. She and Vera were an excellent distraction.

She couldn't forget about Jake, though—the image of his wide jaw and strong mouth seemed to thrum behind her eyelids, each breath including a moment devoted to either thinking of him or trying not to. But besides those few seconds, she was completely engaged with the girls and their stories of how their summer had gone. *Mom took us to the zoo. Vera got lost, but I was the one who got in trouble, which wasn't fair. Do you think that's fair? What's this worm? Why is it doing that? Can you teach fifth? You should teach fifth. I don't want Mrs. Mackie. Why can't you just switch with her? What are you doing with that board over there? Can I try sanding?*

A clicking of heels came down the garden paving stones, and Felicia poked her head around the gate. "Hey, you ready to talk some wedding planning? Oh! You have help!"

Zora looked down at the pile of weeds at her knees. She enjoyed weeding so much better than sanding the cutting board. While Vera pulled more

carrots than weeds, Zora tidied the rest of the tomatoes. Clean dirt under her fingernails was always a
good feeling. "Do I have to help with the plans?"

"Yes. You do. Don't you want some say in this
thing?"

"Why bother?"

Felicia looked at her over an imaginary pair of
reading glasses. "Come again?"

"It isn't real. It isn't my actual wedding. Why do
I have to plan it, too?"

"Because weddings are fun."

Zora had been a bridesmaid in three friends'
weddings. At each, she had gone home alone, as
she'd wanted to. At another wedding of a colleague,
she'd gotten too drunk and had thrown up in an
azalea bush and had had to get a ride home with the
minister. "Weddings aren't fun for anyone, when
you think about it."

Felicia sat in the Adirondack Zora had vacated
and elegantly crossed her legs. She tilted her head.
"Tell me more."

She reminded herself of all the things she'd felt
for years. "They make the couple feel terrible for
spending money they can't afford to start these lives
together, and half of them won't even stay together.
No matter what their big day ends up being, it
won't live up to the hype they've put into planning
it, so they'll be slightly disappointed. And for the

people who come to the wedding, the day reminds them of what they don't have. Single people feel lonely. Married people feel like they've lost the spark the couple getting married obviously has. No one enjoys weddings."

"I love weddings. I love everything about them."

"You're the only one. At the last three weddings I attended, the flower girl either threw up or threw a tantrum. Even *they* don't like them."

"I was a flower girl!" shouted Vera. "I was a flower girl!"

Felicia's eyes lit up. "Oh, you sweet thing. Would you like to do it again?"

Petra put down the cutting board and said, "My sister isn't allowed to talk to strangers, and I'm pretty sure she's not allowed to be in weddings of strangers."

"Not a stranger, darling, this will be Miss Zora's wedding."

There wasn't a moment's hesitation. "Then *I* want to be the flower girl, not Vera."

"Honey, why don't you and Vera move these weeds to the compost pile while I talk with Felicia?" After the girls had trotted off, carrying dead weeds like bridal bouquets, Zora said, "And still no. Not even with them. I don't need to plan a thing. Consider me the easiest-to-please bride ever. What's the opposite of Bridezilla? Bambi Bride?'

"You're made of stone. You just don't care. I get it."

Zora managed a weak smile. "Can't you just organize it for us? Or ask Jake? If he has opinions, he can tell you what he wants. You're right, I do not care." The lie hurt—strangely, after all her protesting, she *did* care. She didn't want a big dress, a big cake, a big deal. Suddenly, she knew that she wanted a simple dress, a homemade cake, a small but significant deal, brightly filled with love.

She wanted Jake at the end of that aisle.

*Oh, Lord have mercy.*

Felicia leaned left and looked around the edge of the gate into the garden. "Let's ask him now."

It was just getting worse, wasn't it?

Then, there he was, all tall and broad and wide, and smiling right at her. Like he'd never seen anything better in his life. Zora almost wanted to look over her shoulder to see exactly what he was looking at—was it the girls running through the raised bed of dahlias?—but she knew it was her. She was the one putting that look on his face, and she could feel the same lightness brightening her own.

Zora was confused as hell, but it all got better the moment she saw him.

He leaned down and kissed her full on the mouth. Zora gasped under his lips as his electricity brought it all back to her. All of it, all of him. Her lower lip quivered as he pulled away his mouth, and her insides heated.

Next to her, Felicia gave a quiet laugh.

Jake straightened up from the kiss. "Ask me what?"

Zora cleared her throat. "Felicia wants you to plan the wedding with her."

Felicia held up a hand. "Wait—"

"Me?"

"I don't want to."

"But—it's our wedding."

"Our fake wedding."

He gave her a smile. "Well, she sure as hell can't plan the real one."

Super-heated confusion rolled through Zora's chest. "Sure. Yeah. So you two should talk."

Jake tilted his head. "You honestly don't care about the details?"

"It's for the network. Not for me. Not for us." The word *us* felt right in her mouth, a warm marble of joy that she didn't know what to do with. So she swallowed it, and her stomach heated, too. *Us.*

"Well, I don't care, either. Felicia, can't your team just handle it? We'll show up—isn't that enough?"

Felicia looked at her phone. "Fine. I'll put Nancy on it. Now, Zora, it's time to take you for a dress fitting."

Oh, boy. Zora should have seen this coming, but she hadn't.

Jake's eyebrows leaped. "A wedding dress fitting?"

Felicia said, "What else, darling? We need to get some shots of Zora trying them on, and try as she might, she can't get out of this one."

"I want to come," said Jake.

Zora turned, hands on hips. "You don't mean it. That you want to come to watch me try on dresses." How hilarious would that be? Her trying white foofy dresses on in front of him?

Felicia snorted. "Don't be silly."

"Why not? It's not our real wedding, so why can't I see the dress beforehand?"

Felicia frowned. "I know this is non-traditional and a total setup, but you *do* like each other. You sure you want to jinx that?"

"Wait," said Zora. "I don't mind." It *wouldn't* be a real wedding dress—it was just a costume. It might be fun. A laugh. He might actually be helpful. Nerves lit under her skin, excited jolts.

"Great." Jake rocked back on his heels. "Can't wait. Can we go now?"

## TWENTY-EIGHT

It was fun until it wasn't.

When she tried on the first dress, Zora laughed until her sides ached, and Jake had joined her. She'd picked the laciest, floofiest, beruffledest, *giganticest* dress in the whole store to try on. Felicia had said the network would approve anything that she liked, so she didn't even glance at price tags.

With the help of the saleswoman named Lois— a tiny, older woman wearing a skintight black dress, no smile, and no makeup—Zora wriggled into the concoction. She managed to keep herself together until she swanned out of the dressing room. Tony was using the Steadicam, and Anna was doing sound, but *both* of them cracked up as they saw her.

"*I'm* the belle of the ball," she announced,

turning sideways to make it past a hanging rack of dresses.

Felicia gave a shriek of laughter.

Jake just grinned and said, "Why, Miss Scarlet, as I live and breathe."

The boning of the corset cut into her ribs, but Zora had to admit, even though it was hilarious, there was something completely delicious about the way Jake seemed unable to take his eyes off the tops of her breasts. They were pushed up so high and looked so ripe that she'd almost been embarrassed to come out of the dressing room. Now she was grateful she had.

He could look at her all day like that, and she'd just happily stand here while he did it.

As if he could hear her thoughts, he said, "I could look at you all day." His voice was hoarse, and he jumped when Tony guffawed at him.

Zora moved her hips. The miles of fabric dipped and swayed with a *shuushing* sound. "It's actually pretty fun to wear. Like the heaviest and prettiest costume I ever put on."

Lois's voice was brisk. "There, now. You've had your fun. This obviously isn't the dress for you."

Felicia said, "But is it America's dress? Would they love this one? You do look like someone covered in white fondant, so there's that."

Jake shifted in his seat. "It's gorgeous. *You're* gorgeous. But it's not you."

It all crashed back onto her then—this wasn't about her. This was the show, and it was all a sham. "That doesn't matter, does it? It's all fake—shouldn't I just get the biggest, most expensive one?"

Jake just blinked. Then he looked at the ground.

Lois's eyebrows flew upward. "Fake?"

"She didn't mean that." Felicia patted Lois's arm. "Zora just believes that weddings as a whole are an overpriced commodity in an already overwhelmed capitalist market. It's just economics. Don't worry, Lois. You have some others for us to try, right? Happiest day of their lives, and all that!"

"Follow me, please." Lois still didn't approve.

Zora couldn't blame her.

Five dresses later, Zora was seriously over the gown thing. Ruffles, beads, and sequins—each dress blingier than the next. Each time she moved into the waiting lounge to be filmed, the crew joked about her climbing to the top of a wedding cake. With every dress, the whole thing became less funny, though she forced herself to laugh. Tony and Anna seemed to be honestly enjoying themselves. Felicia, too.

She was not.

And from the look on Jake's face, the way he

smiled but his eyes didn't match, Zora didn't think he was having fun anymore, either.

Down to her plain white bra and underwear yet again, she turned to Lois, who was carrying in two more cakelike creations. The small woman was barely visible under them. "Here we go, you're going to love this one by—"

"Please. Lois. Help me."

Lois carefully deposited the dresses onto the empty rack. She turned neatly, her hands on her hips. She'd been professional so far, but now her voice sounded real. "Are you going to tell me what's going on?"

Weakly, Zora said, "It's like Felicia said. It's a TV show."

"But you have feelings for him. Real ones. I can tell."

"Well..."

"My whole career is built on how brides feel. Don't even try to lie to me. We've gone through the expensive dresses that your boss wanted you to try on. Are you ready to tell me what *you* want now?"

Zora nodded.

Five minutes later, she stared into the mirror.

"Damn it." Her voice came out in a whisper.

Behind her, Lois fastened the last hook. "Yes. I know."

"Do I have to go out there? Jake will..."

"I still don't approve of him seeing you before the day, TV show or no. But yes, you do. Go out there."

Zora took one more look. This was her dress. She recognized it like she did her own voice. It was a simple piece of off-white raw silk. It had narrow straps and a neckline that plunged far past what would normally be comfortable but still somehow kept her covered. It skimmed her hips and hung in lacy wisps just past her knee. It was almost like a nightgown, if a nightgown could make her feel like she could go to a party in Paris or New York. She looked different in it. She looked...beautiful.

She cleared her throat. "What shoes would go with this?"

"A simple silk ballet flat, perhaps. Or just like that." Lois pointed at her bare feet.

"I think you're right."

"Go show them."

Felicia and Tony and Anna were all there when she padded into the lounge, but it was as if they were hidden by mist.

There seemed to be no one there but Jake.

She walked slowly to the middle of the room, to the spot under the lamps where she'd twirled and laughed in all the other dresses. She wasn't laughing now.

"What do you think?" There was only one

person she was asking.

Jake only said, "I..."

He appeared flummoxed, as if someone had just told him that the world wasn't round, or that his name wasn't actually his name.

"You like it?" She felt naked suddenly, and essentially, she was. Why hadn't she ever noticed how nude she was inside her clothes? Especially this dress. It was just air and a few molecules—nothing to shield her from his gaze. Not that she wanted anything to.

"You look..." His throat sounded tight, and he didn't appear to be able to finish his sentence. "That's the one."

"Well." She looked down at her bare feet and the chipped pink polish. If this were her real wedding, this *would* be the one.

And so would he.

Shit.

She spun. "I'm not sure. I'll try a few more. Lois—"

"We need to talk." Jake was right behind her. "Lois, can we have a minute?"

"Of course," said Lois. Zora didn't look at her, but Lois sounded pleased. Some help she was.

"Let me take this off before we talk." They were already down the hall and halfway into the dressing room.

He followed her in without asking.

She should protest.

But she didn't want to.

"Don't take that off." Jake's voice was a warning.

She understood the warning right to her bones, but she still wanted to hear him say it. "Why not?"

"Because I won't be responsible for my actions."

She felt a rush of heat and a slipperiness between her thighs, just like that. Neither of them should be responsible for their actions. He should rip off the dress and press her up against the wall of the dressing room—God. Zora pushed her hair back and tried to pull a full breath into her lungs. "What did you want to talk to me about?" She was proud that her voice didn't shake.

In answer, he kissed her. His mouth on hers was hot, a wildfire set in a canyon. In a moment, the dress would scorch and turn brown, she knew it. There was nothing that could withstand this heat for long.

She kissed him back with everything she had inside her, trying to put into the kiss what she felt, whatever the hell that was. His tongue was what she wanted, what she needed, but she desperately needed it to go further, lower, to give her more...

But Jake pulled back. He looked into her eyes. And he named it.

"I love you," he said.

TWENTY-NINE

The words came out of Jake's mouth as naturally as if he'd said them to her a million times before. He wanted to say them that many, so he might as well start catching up now. "Zora, I love you."

"I *heard* you."

It wasn't the answer he was hoping for, but her eyes said more than her lips did.

He touched her cheek. She caught his hand and pressed a kiss into his palm, a shockingly intimate gesture. It shook him even more than her kiss had. The ground beneath his feet rolled as if he were standing on his boat on a stormy day.

"I'm serious," he said. "This isn't about the show. This has gone way past the show."

"I know."

"What do we do about it?"

"That, I *don't* know."

He slid his hand up into her hair. The nape of her neck was slippery with sweat that he wanted to lick away. "I want to marry you."

Zora pulled slightly away and glanced into the mirror. "It's just the dress. I want to marry myself in this thing."

She was trying to break the mood, but he wasn't going to let her. "I want to marry you for good. For keeps."

A sigh was his answer. She didn't meet his eyes.

"Zora, I've loved you since I met you, so long ago."

"Since then?" She turned more, so that he could only see her face in the mirror. "Come on, Jake. We were kids."

"Well, we were smart kids. Tell me you didn't feel the same way."

She was silent.

"Come on, Zora. Tell me you're not in love with me. If you can say it, I'll try to believe you." She wouldn't say it—she couldn't. He could feel from here that she felt the same way.

"You're leaving."

"I'll stay."

She blew out a sharp breath. "Then I'm making you stay, and you'll regret it."

"I don't think I'd regret anything about you. I never have, and I doubt I ever will. Besides, you have summer vacations. We can sail then and stay here otherwise."

"You've *never* wanted roots here."

It was true. He hadn't. What if he'd grown them without even noticing, though?

She went on. "I don't like the ocean."

But he'd seen her on the surfboard, and he felt her in his arms on the boat. "You could learn to like it."

She didn't speak, but something darker crossed her face. Jake didn't understand it, but he knew there was more. "What is it?"

"Nothing," she said, crossing her arms.

"You're hiding something from me. These are just excuses you're giving me." He paused, and she closed her eyes. "Please, Zora, have that much respect for me."

Her face looked tortured, her eyes bleak. "I can't have children."

The words didn't even make sense. They weren't talking about children. "What?"

"I'm infertile." Her voice cracked.

Wait a second. How did this fit with her not being able to tell him that she loved him? "I'm not following here."

"You deserve children."

His brain spun. "I can honestly tell you that kids are the furthest thing from my mind right now."

Her cheeks were bright red, and her mouth was tight. "You want them. You've said it."

Jake racked his brain and couldn't remember the last time he'd even thought about wanting kids, let alone spoken a desire for them aloud. "I feel like you're just changing the subject." He caught her hand and kept his voice low. "Tell me you don't love me, and I swear to God, I'll march out of here and forget all of this ever happened. That night that we shared on the boat, the way you look at me... The feeling I get when I'm near you like you're my forever. Just tell me you don't feel the same way."

Zora squeezed his hand and then, as if the motion had been involuntary, pulled it back. "You remember when I broke up with you?"

*No.* He did *not* remember that—oh, she meant back in high school. "Of course I do. You were my first heartbreak."

She gave a small smile. "You were mine, too. I broke up with you because I'd gotten pregnant."

"You what?" He could hear the blood rushing in his head. They'd been careful, hadn't they? Had he been that idiotic a kid?

"A condom must have broken. The pregnancy was ectopic."

Jake shook his head hoping to clear it. "I don't know what that is."

"It means the fetus starts growing in the fallopian tube. If it continues to grow, it can kill the mother."

"Oh, my God." Glacial water coursed through his veins.

"And in my case, I just didn't know what was happening until it was too late. The surgery went wrong, and I almost died. I had to have a hysterectomy. It was so bad I lost everything, both ovaries and all. When my mother said I was getting my gallbladder out, she was lying."

She'd almost *died?* She'd gone through all that alone? Without him? "You should have told me."

"No, I didn't. I needed *not* to tell you. You wanted kids—I was too young to know much, but I knew that would be a deal breaker. I knew that your brothers were everything to you, and that you'd want the cookie-cutter family, too." She yanked her hair back and pulled it into a ponytail using a rubber band she took off her wrist. "They tried to save my second ovary and tube, but there was an infection."

"But..." This was impossible. He had to go back in time and fix it, but he couldn't—he just had to stand here, now, powerless.

"It's not a big deal for me, really. I've never felt

that biological clock ticking. Sometimes I've wondered if it's because I can't do it—maybe I lost the clock along with my fertility."

"Zora—" His voice shook.

She held up her hands. "Anyway, it is what it is. I'm not sad about it. My life is pretty great, and my students really are my children. Each year I get a new batch, and each year, I feel luckier than ever. I have more kids than anyone I know, and I love every single one of them. But you, you deserve more."

Him? *He* deserved more? He was the problem here. His gut clenched, and his stomach felt queasy. "I'm so sorry." Goddamn. And he'd never known. He would have done anything—

She went on. "I can't believe I went along with this. I just wanted the house—I wasn't thinking about what it would *mean*. To both of us." Her voice broke. "We can't talk about love. This is business. My house. Your trip."

His trip? His trip meant nothing, not when he wanted to stay right here, with her. The worst part was that he'd *hurt* her and he'd never known. "I hurt you. I permanently damaged you."

"My body hurt itself. Nothing to do with you."

It *was* to do with him. The fact that they'd had sex was the reason she couldn't carry a child. And that was a goddamn tragedy. He could imagine her so clearly with a baby—his baby—on her hip. She'd look like a goddess of fertility.

But she wasn't one. She was infertile, and it was his fault. "You should have told me, though."

Zora faced him and squared her shoulders. "It wasn't your business."

"It was my baby. It was my fault."

"Bullshit." Suddenly, the dress no longer made her look virginal and bridelike. The way it clung to her body and dripped to her calves made her look like a warrior, about to don leather armor. Her gaze was fierce, and her stance was strong. "It wasn't a baby. Don't call it that. It was an embryo that was trying to kill me. Don't turn that into me doing something morally wrong."

"Oh, *God*. You did nothing wrong!"

"You don't have to convince me of that. I know that."

That wasn't what he'd meant at all. *He'd* been the one in the wrong. He should have fought her on the breakup—should have insisted on knowing what wasn't working. Instead, he'd been a typical guy, and he'd gone out and gotten another girlfriend. One that he hadn't cared about at all. Jake hadn't cared about any woman—ever—the way he'd always felt about her.

He was screwing up in three hundred different ways right now. How did he fix this? He needed a different angle, and he needed it instantly.

"Zora, I will promise you right here and right now that I'll spend the rest of my life making up for this. You never know what medical miracles have been invented since then." Goddammit, there was nothing science could do to help her without the raw material she'd lost. Why had he said that? "Or we can adopt. We can do whatever you want. I just need you to know that I'm in. I'm all in. I'll help you through all of this."

Zora's eyes were so wide he felt he might drown in them. "You have no—"

She broke off as Felicia's voice called over the door, "Hey, you two, how's it going in there? Zora, honey, that's the best dress I've ever seen on a bride. Shall I tell her we'll take it?"

"No!" Zora shouted. "I hate it. Pick something poofy in my size."

"Seriously?"

"The more rhinestones, the better." Zora pointed at the dressing room door. "Jake, get out."

"But—"

"Go away." She crossed her arms awkwardly as if trying to hide her chest. Or her heart.

Goddammit, he'd made her feel uncomfortable. Maybe even unsafe. *Again.* "Zora—"

She cut him off. "What you asked me earlier? If I could tell you I didn't love you?"

His chest hurt. "Yeah?"

"I don't. I didn't then, and I don't now. This is just about getting the house I want. You want to sail away and have kids somewhere someday. I just want a home."

She was lying. He could tell. She was sacrificing herself for something, but he didn't understand what. His body felt cold, and his vision narrowed.

Wasn't she lying?

What if she wasn't?

If she wasn't lying, and he kept pushing her, then he was everything he detested in a person.

"Go," she said one last time, and she made it sound final.

He went.

# THIRTY

The next week, it turned out that Zora had a talent she'd never known about—she could act her way through pain even with a heart that kept threatening to quit beating. She could talk with her mother and make jokes with her friends. She could even work on the house while on camera with the rebuild crew and not make too many mistakes.

She managed to avoid Jake as she worked. It was as if she'd obtained Jake-sonar while she'd been helping build the new cabinets in the kitchen. Without even seeing him, she could feel when he was approaching. When she felt it, she slipped out the other way.

The worst part had been the way he'd *looked* at her that day in the dressing room, even before she lied to him. He'd looked at her as if she were less-than. She couldn't have children, and she'd known that since she was eighteen, and she was fine with it, body and soul.

But instead of believing that she was okay with it, he'd looked at her like she was something he'd dropped and broken and couldn't put back together again.

She wasn't a house hit by a car. She wasn't something he could bang with a hammer (or anything else, for that matter) and fix.

Her womb was gone, that was all. Everything else did. But judging by the way his face had fallen to the floor, that wasn't going to be enough for him, even if he wanted it to be.

Lying to him about never loving him was the only thing she could hit him with. And it had worked.

*You should give him a chance,* her mother had said.

*It's a fake game show. None of it matters,* she'd snapped back. *He doesn't need a chance. We need to finish it up and get paid.*

A much bigger problem was that at the moment he'd told her he loved her in a dressing room, she'd known one thing for sure. She loved him back, and probably always had.

But...

Jake felt *sorry* for her, which was probably a natural response. It was still one hundred percent totally unacceptable. So she'd lied.

He should get on his boat and with the show money, sail off over the horizon. Maybe lying to him would help him to do that.

The thing was, every time she thought about him sailing away, she got this hot, strange twist in her chest as if her heart—soggy with stupid, hot tears that came when she tried to sleep—was trying to wring itself out.

The time sped past, Felicia in charge of all the details because Zora refused to make decisions for an elaborate ruse of a party. She hadn't even thought about a rehearsal dinner, but Felicia had insisted. "Viewers will want to see every bit we feed them. They'll *die* to see it on screen."

She'd begged to skip it, but *apparently*, the fake bride couldn't skip the fake night before the fake wedding.

So, for an hour now, she'd sat next to Jake and laughed at people's toasts. The rehearsal dinner was at the Crab's Claw, and it seemed like half the town was there. Everyone wanted to stand at the mic and say something to them. If someone made a toast, part of it might make it onto the show, and Darling Bay was full of people who wanted to be on national television.

She and Jake spoke when they had to, around mountains of words that couldn't be said. Jake leaned close to reach for the wine bottle, and she could smell him—soap and mint and vanilla. And she felt like she was dying inside. Zora was in love with a man who would only ever see her as broken, as something he had to make up for. Yes, he'd fallen in love with her before he'd known her broken state, but that didn't matter anymore because now he knew. Guilt swamped her, and she pushed back tears she refused to let get caught on camera.

He *thought* he loved her. She knew she loved him. And *none* of this would ever work. It couldn't. He felt sorry for her, and that was nothing to base a relationship on. Especially when Jake's whole purpose in life was to leave.

She had to marry him, for real, on camera, all with the intention of getting a divorce in a few months. Felicia said they should live together for those first months, but when Zora had pushed back, Felicia had held up her hands. "We can't make you do anything. We can only suggest."

That was a crock. She'd only said that because it wasn't actually in the contract addendum they'd signed, the only thing they'd forgotten to add in. Thank God.

With the cameras focused on her and Jake, she grinned as a local drunk named Norma held up her whiskey sour. "These crazy kids are finally getting hitched. Here's to them making sweet whoopie in every time zone out on that dang boat of Jake's."

Zora rolled her eyes as cheerfully as she could with that big fat smile plastered to her face and poured herself a little more wine. Her head was pounding, and her throat was dry.

Norma kept talking.

Jake said, "Do you think this night will ever end?"

Zora shook her head brightly and laughed. "No!" Anyone watching them would think they were laughing over a private joke, and while the show would be picking up their conversation over the mics, there was no way they'd play what they were actually saying. "This night will last forever!" She gave another cubic zirconia smile and clinked her glass against his. They posed together as Domenico took their picture for the *Gazette*.

"We've got to do something."

The tone of his voice made her nervous, but she agreed—she was about to burst out of her skin if this went on much longer.

Jake gestured at Norma, who'd been talking this whole time about alternate places to make whoopie. "Norma, sorry to interrupt, and I agree with everything you're saying, but can I borrow the mic?"

Norma looked pleased to have a task. "Why,

yes, indeedy! Here I come!" She weeble-wobbled her way to them and held out the microphone. Extending her moment as long as she could, she said into it, "Here you are, dear boy. Celebrate your love with your whole bodies, as often as you can. Don't forget, God made us naked for a reason."

Zora's whole face went hot as she found she was unable to get the image of Jake's naked body out of her mind. That man *was* made naked for a very good reason.

And it wasn't fair.

Jake stood and held the mic to his lips. "Hello." Feedback filled the room, a squeal that made everyone put their hands to their ears. After Nate fixed it and the sound stopped, Jake cleared his throat audibly over the mic.

"Sorry. I guess I'm nervous. Some of you might have heard I'm getting married tomorrow." A ripple of light laughter swept the room. "I've never been a groom before, and it's essential to me to get it right. I know this whole thing looks weird. You all had to sign waivers just to get your dinners tonight, and cameras have been busting into your conversations. I apologize for that."

His voice got stronger. "But I have to say something really important, and no, it can't wait until I'm watching her walk toward me and the minister. I've got to say it now, just so that this woman hears me loud and clear." He turned so that he was facing her.

Zora's face went hot, and sweat trickled down her back. Every camera in the room was trained on her, including dozens of cell phones people held overhead. She caught her mother and Tuesday exchanging satisfied glances.

"Zora Nelson, I'm only getting married once, and it's happening tomorrow. I'm only marrying one woman in this lifetime, and I'm only marrying the one I'm head over heels in love with. I asked you twice to marry me, once off camera, and once on. You gave me the same answer both times, but that *yes* I got in the ocean, when no one could hear us, that was the one that mattered to me." He paused, his eyes the darkest blue she'd ever seen. "This is a *real* wedding. This isn't for the show, and everyone watching, both here and in the world should know that. You're the reason my heart beats in the morning. You always have been. I've never been able to settle down, and I've never been able to leave. Now I know why. I was waiting for you to see me again. I love you."

Jake leaned down. She felt his lips on hers at the same moment she felt dampness on her cheek—it took her a moment to realize she was crying. But she still couldn't say it back to him. Instead, she tried to say with her kiss what she felt inside—love tinged with sadness over the fact that this simply couldn't work.

Because, of course, they wouldn't make it. They couldn't. He didn't love her—he just felt sorry for her, and maybe he felt guilty, though he shouldn't. The ectopic pregnancy had just been one of those things. He was confusing those emotions with love.

Zora *had* to let go of any hope that she might hold deep in her heart that things might end differently, might end well. She looked over the crowd and saw nothing but happy expressions.

Mallory's face. Even she wore a bright smile as she gave Zora an earnest-looking thumbs-up.

God. She'd been wrong even about Mallory. How could she trust herself to understand anything? She couldn't understand her own heart, which was probably just as trustworthy as her understanding.

Why *had* Zora kept the truth about the pregnancy from him? What might have been different if she had just told him? Maybe they'd still be together, with two gorgeous, adopted kids. Maybe he would have taken off immediately for sunny climes on the *Kerplunk*.

It was her fault that they'd never know the truth.

She couldn't say that she loved him—if she did, she'd screw something else up and break both their hearts all over again. And maybe if she didn't say it, it wouldn't be true.

So Zora kissed him instead of answering. She put both hands on either side of his face and tried to memorize the contours of his cheeks, the way his jaw felt under her fingers, all while putting the love she wouldn't speak into that one, long, perfect, heartrending kiss.

Someone shouted, "To Jake and Zora!"

Then someone else yelled, "To all the beautiful babies you'll make!"

Zora just hoped her tears would read as happy ones on the screen.

# THIRTY-ONE

The next morning dawned dark, a thing that was rare in August in Darling Bay. Jake felt hungover and slightly queasy, though he'd only had two glasses of wine at the rehearsal dinner.

It was okay. The day would brighten up. It always did. It *was* summer, after all.

But *he* didn't seem to be able to brighten. A sense of foreboding hung over his shoulders like a pall of smoke.

When he drank his coffee on deck, he didn't like the way the boat rocked. It wasn't heavy fog—this was the threat of real rain. The wedding was going to be out of doors, of course. No one got married indoors in Darling Bay. But it wouldn't be at the beach, like most local weddings. Zora had suggested it be on school grounds. It was the only idea he'd heard her contribute to the wedding planning, but he would have been on board anyway. The slight rise of the playing field, all green grass and sycamores, had one open side to the west. The ocean glimmered in the distance from there, a perfect view for kids playing (though he preferred the view to the south, her kids' garden and the gate that led to her house).

It would be a beautiful wedding if it didn't storm.

Mallory came above deck and waved. "Good luck today, tiger!" A man, someone he didn't know, followed at her footsteps, carrying two mugs of coffee. She looked happy, her hair a mess. Good for her. She deserved happiness. Hopefully, she'd get that guy to settle down with her using no form of entrapment other than her long blond hair and admittedly sweet nature.

"I winked at your girl last night right after your speech," Mallory said. "She looked like she was going to pass out, but I could see her feelings right there on her face."

"Yeah?" Maybe Mallory had seen something he hadn't. "What did you see?"

"Sheer terror. Mixed with love."

Hope rose thinly. "Really?"

Mallory nodded, then looked over her shoulder

at the man who'd seated himself on the foredeck. "Sorry about the way I acted. You know."

The pregnancy test. Jake felt tired inside. "It's okay." It hadn't been, but whatever.

"I just hope she knows how big a catch you are." Mallory gave a wave and sat next to the man, kissing him on the ear.

Was he, though?

Jake took a shower and shaved. Felicia and the crew had his tux and shoes and everything else he needed at the school. They'd even have his bride.

*Damn it.*

It didn't feel right. Zora just hadn't been *present* the night before. She'd been faking, and in a real way, so had he. Confusion was the thing he felt most strongly this morning. The only certitude he had was that he wanted to slip a ring on Zora's finger, and right now it wasn't even for the right reason.

He wanted to own her, to make her understand that he loved her and that they were meant to be together. And honestly, that was bullshit. What kind of an asshole wanted to own someone?

Him, for one.

He strode through the marina, a scowl on his face. He didn't need coffee, and he wouldn't need a sandwich for later—the network had arranged for Lydia St. Clair to do the catering, so the food would be amazing. But he needed to bounce some of this energy off someone who wasn't related to him. Liam and Aidan wanted to be done with the show, and they wanted him to get the money to sail away. They weren't going to help him make hard decisions.

But Humphrey and Bogart—they'd tell him the truth.

"Dead man walking!" trumpeted Bogart as Jake stepped out of the wind into Darling Bait.

"That's what they say," said Jake.

"Coffee?" Humphrey held up a blackened pot.

"I'm good."

"Are you?" Bogart leaned his sweatered elbows on the glass counter. "Because you look like hell, son."

"I feel like it, too."

Humphrey gestured out to the dark parking lot. "Maybe it'll clear up later."

From living on the water for years, Jake knew the weather in his bones, and these two men knew it ten times better than he did. They were more reliable than the weather channel. "You know it won't."

"Sometimes life hands you a squall on the most important day. Get through this, and you'll get through anything."

"They're putting up an arbor with things attached to it." Jake hadn't really been listening when

Felicia and the decorator were talking about tulle and roses, but he knew one thing: that wasn't going to go well.

"Yeah, that'll fly away. It's at the school, right?"

Jake nodded.

Humphrey swallowed some of his coffee and said, "You'd do well to move it into the multipurpose room."

Bogart said brightly, "Getting married with the smell of fish sticks and tater tots. Nothing finer."

"We're doomed," said Jake. And they probably were. Zora hadn't believed a word he'd said the night before. He could read the truth in her kiss—she didn't have a single hope for them.

"The whole thing is a fake." The words came out before he could stop them. To keep his hands busy, he picked up a greenish-blue fishing fly. He spun it in his fingers. "That's the reason the network has fixed up Denny's house so fast. She gets to keep it. I get a shit-ton of money. I can afford to go on my trip. The show's canceled. This is just the big finale. The biggest, fakest of all fake finales."

Humphrey looked surprised, his wide eyes going even wider. But Bogart just nodded his balding head. "Figured," he said.

"Huh?"

"Known Zora and her mom a long time. Apple don't fall far from that tree. Camille likes to be safe at home. Zora's not going to sail away to Micronesia with you. She wants to stay here and have babies."

"She doesn't want kids."

Humphrey shook his head. "All women want kids."

"She says she doesn't. Says her kids at school are all she needs."

"She's lying," said Humphrey. "My first wife said that, but then she got knocked up by the butcher and left me, pretty happy about it."

Bogart lifted a thick gray eyebrow. "Might not have been about the kid."

Humphrey said, "Do *you* want kids?"

"That's the thing. I used to think someday I'd want to settle down and have some, but that's because I thought that's what people did. That's the way you build a life. Liam and Felicia have Timbo and Rosemary. Aidan and Tuesday have their little girl. Isn't that what you're *supposed* to do?"

"Supposed to?" Humphrey got out a small flask and dumped something clear into his coffee then held it out to Jake. "Snort?"

Though he was tempted, he shook his head. "Yeah, supposed to. I mean, it's like a house, right? You don't build a house without a frame. Supports. You can't paint the inside until the drywall's hung. You have to do things in order, like falling in love and getting married. Then you have kids. That's what I've always thought."

"Good grief, you're not very smart, are you?"

"Hey!"

"Life never goes the way you expect it to."

Bogart nodded. "You think I planned to hold up this counter for the last twenty years of my life, talking to my friend here? No way. I thought I'd be living in Aruba with a nubile twenty-year-old. But I like it here just fine. It's okay to not want kids."

He knew that, consciously. Then, what was bothering him? "But what if she really wants kids and isn't admitting it?" That was it. That was why he was so upset. It wasn't about him—it was about the fact that Zora was a born mother, and he'd broken her. Unintentionally, of course. "And she didn't tell me about what happened to her." That was maybe the worst part. She'd kept it from him. It shouldn't have been a secret. She shouldn't have been left with that burden. She should have told the *truth*.

"She said her school kids are all the children she needs?" asked Humphrey.

"Yeah."

Bogart looked at Humphrey. Humphrey looked at Bogart. Both shook their heads.

"What?"

Humphrey was the one who spoke, after a long,

slow sip of his doctored coffee. "If she tells you something and you choose to disbelieve it? Son, you're not ready for marriage."

Shit. "What should I do?"

"Listen. And watch. And trust."

What if Jake was a bad listener? What if he didn't see what he should? What if he couldn't trust his own gut?

"Does she love you?" asked Bogart.

"She won't tell me if she does or not. Guys, I'm in a panic here." Sweat broke out at his hairline, and his chest tightened. Was he doing this for all the wrong reasons? He needed to get out of his head, out of his heart for just a damned second. He took a shaky breath. If she didn't love him, then at least he was giving her the gift of the house she loved. Right? Oh, God. "Am I having a heart attack, maybe?"

Humphrey raised his mug to him. "It's your wedding day, son. It's only going to get worse."

# THIRTY-TWO

Nothing, not one single thing, had gone right so far.

Zora had barely closed her eyes all night, and when she finally did, after five in the morning, she'd overslept. Camille had been no help, staying in bed to watch the news. "I thought you needed your rest," was all she said when Zora asked why she hadn't woken her.

Her cell phone hadn't taken a charge, so even though the show had called her, it hadn't rung. Zora was supposed to be in hair and makeup by ten a.m. but slid into the chair almost an hour late. The network had borrowed her own classroom, and it was bizarre to see mirrors propped on her whiteboard, and a full salon set up where her science bookcase usually stood. When the hair stylist made her first wave with the flat iron, a terrible smell rose into the air. The iron had overheated and some of Zora's hair had singed right before the iron gave a little popping explosion and died. The burned bit was hidden now under a nest of pinned-up, hair-sprayed tendrils, but the smell wouldn't leave Zora's nose.

The makeup artist was the same one who'd made her up for the first day of shooting.

"No," said Zora when she saw her coming. She held up her hands. "Not like you did last time. I want natural."

The young woman rubbed at an obviously new and angry neck tattoo. "No problem. I get you."

When she'd spun around to face the mirror, Zora could only laugh because crying would be too exhausting.

Dark eyeliner and bright pink eyeshadow made her look like a goth going to communion. Her lips were a bold red which might have actually worked had the blush not been a contrasting peach.

Even Felicia had looked startled. "Darling... I'm not quite sure that's you. Anna, what do you think?"

The camera woman's face had said it all.

"That's it," said Zora. "I'm starting over."

"It's not that bad," protested Felicia. "Maybe we

can wipe off the blush and a little of the eyeliner. We do want you to have some color for the camera."

Zora whirled. "I haven't had color this whole show after that first morning when I looked like a hooker. I'm a pale and boring person." She heard the camera zoom in. She would *never* be able to watch this show. "I'm just going to stick to boring and pale. If Jake doesn't like it, he can marry someone else."

The words stung, but not as much as the powdered soap and the cold water she used in the girls' bathroom to wash her face. She dried her skin on the rough paper towels. Then she tugged out as many bobby pins from her head as she could grab. She brushed out the curls. The singed hair would just have to be visible until she could get to her hair stylist, Carol, next week. She slicked on the raisin lipstick she wore when she was feeling fancy and called it good.

Jake liked her this way.

He loved her this way. Oh, *goddammit*. He *loved* her.

And she loved him.

The thin light coming in the frosted window got even darker. She checked her cell. Less than half an hour until she was supposed to walk down the aisle.

The bathroom door slammed open, and Tuesday stood there, dressed in a long lavender strapless gown. "The decorated arbor they set up keeps almost lifting off the ground. You should see what the tulle is doing in that wind. Every time they set up the chairs, they blow over. It's like a hurricane out there."

Zora had never been gladder to see someone. "It's like a hurricane in *here*. What are you doing in that dress?"

"Felicia got us. You know, the brother thing. I have to say, Aidan in a tux is something else. We barely made it here on time, if you know what I mean. Liam and Felicia look good, too."

"I'm in hell." Zora backed up and dropped the lid of a toilet to sit down in her jeans. She'd have to change into the dress soon, and then it would be real.

"If by hell you mean you're about to get married to the man you're in love with, then I hope more people experience this particular kind of devastation. You do look pretty sick, though. Are you going to hurl?"

*The man you're in love with.* "Probably."

Tuesday propped a hip on the low sink. "At least you're not dressed yet. Vomit away."

"Should I do this?" Zora's throat was raw. "Should I go through with the wedding?"

"Oh, sugar, I wish I could tell you. Do you want to?"

Did she want to? Zora had no idea what she wanted. "I signed a contract. The house is almost move-in ready. They gave me my dream." But her dream of Jake...

"Forget all that. Just forget it." Tuesday knelt and took Zora's cold hands in her warm ones. "Let's pretend there was no show. No contract. No house. Just you and Jake. He loves you and has asked you to marry him. You've said yes because you love him, too, obviously."

"*Is* it obvious?"

"Only to anyone who has eyes, yes. So right now, you and I are pretending nothing else exists. Just you and him. Would you walk down the aisle to meet him at the end? And by aisle, I mean a wind tunnel surrounded by flapping tulle and flying roses?"

*Yes*, her heart said. "He deserves more than a woman who can't have kids and doesn't want to spend years on a boat."

Tuesday looked momentarily surprised but recovered quickly. "Do you think he's a grown-ass man who can make his own decisions?"

"Of course."

"And you love him."

God, so much. So terrifyingly much. "Yes." Her heart felt like it might beat right out of her chest. "I love him."

"Then what are you going to do?"

"I'm going to walk through that wind tunnel."

Tuesday nodded. Then she looked at Zora's hair. "Let's work on your hair, though. Maybe we can hide the blackened bits."

# THIRTY-THREE

Jake couldn't ever remember a wind squall like this in summer.

Liam said, "Good thing we're not at the beach with sand flying."

Aidan said, "Global warming."

The three brothers stood in the doorway of the multipurpose room. The reception had already been moved inside, but Felicia hadn't thought a wedding filmed in a room filled with dozens of long tables would be the most gorgeous spot for a wedding the whole country would watch, so she'd kept it outside. Jake couldn't decide if it was a good idea or the worst he'd ever heard.

The guests were being seated. The few women who'd worn hats had either taken them off or had already lost them over the baseball diamond to the north. In the distance, the sea was gray streaked with white foam, and seagulls were flapping inland in flocks. Large speakers were set up in the grass, softly playing classical music. The white arbor really did look like it was about to lift off, even though Felicia's tech guys swore they'd staked it down well.

Felicia, dressed in a floor-length lavender gown, sidled up to them. She smiled gracefully as guests filed past. Liam took her hand without saying anything. Felicia kept her everything's-fine face on, but her voice came out in a squeak. "You guys, I'm freaking *out*."

Jake's heart plummeted. "She backed out. I knew it. I knew that—"

"Stop it. She's fine. Or at least Tuesday says she is—they won't let me in the bathroom, which is only one-eighth of my reason to freak out. No, the minister just texted. His car broke down in Half-Moon Bay. Even if he caught a ride, he wouldn't make it on time."

"Does it matter?" Liam asked. "It's not like they really *need* it to be real. Aren't you still going to get a divorce? This way you won't need one, right? I'll do the wedding if you want to."

Jake started. "Did you hear me last night? I'm only doing this once. This is as freaking real as it gets. We need a legal justice of the peace because I'm marrying that woman today. Period."

Liam looked at first startled and then delighted. "I'll go see what I can do. Good for you, brother."

Felicia didn't look comforted, though. "What if he doesn't find one?"

Aidan said, "Then we fake it."

"No—" started Jake.

Aidan held up a hand. "And then we drive straight to Half-Moon Bay to make it real. But there has to be someone here who can do it. Don't sweat it."

Oh, Jake was sweating it all right.

So was Felicia. For the first time maybe ever, Jake was witnessing Felicia losing her cool. She pressed her hands together in what looked like prayer. "This isn't going to work. We can't have a wedding in a hurricane. This is going to look like a comedy special. How is this going to play as romantic, when we won't be able to hear your vows over the wind in your mics?"

Jake didn't care. As long as Zora could hear him, that was all that mattered. "It'll be fine."

But, of course, it wasn't.

HALF AN HOUR LATER, Jake stood at the end

of the grassy aisle next to his brothers. The wind was colder and stronger now, but he barely felt it.

Soon, she'd be there. Yes, this was crazy. Yes, it was for a reality show which had almost nothing to do with actual reality, but the marriage itself would be as real as the fact that he was in crazy-love with Zora and probably always had been. He couldn't wait to show her that he honest-to-God wanted to spend the rest of their lives together. He wanted to kiss her for the first time as her husband, and he wanted to continue to do so until they drew their last breaths, hopefully at the same time in very, very old age.

Norma had been pressed into ministerial service. Dressed in a shiny yellow muumuu, she didn't quite look like a minister, exactly, but she did look mostly sober. She also looked rather priestly, with her million necklaces that jangled every time she moved, and her monk-like shorn head. She might not play that well on national TV, but Jake didn't care. He loved Norma. She was like family. Better than any hired minister from Half-Moon Bay could ever have been.

"Hey, Jakey," she shout-whispered. "Don't be nervous! I pulled a card right before I got here and got the Ten of Cups! You're going to be the happiest family in the world! Lots and lots of kids!"

Kids? No, no, no. He refused to take that as a

bad sign. He closed his eyes and sent up a prayer to whatever might be listening. *Please, let Zora love me, too.* "Thanks, Norma. I'll take happy."

The music changed and got louder. A Darling Songbird's classic, "Home in You," started. Oh, wow, it wasn't even coming from the speakers—Adele, Molly, and Lana Darling stood in front of a microphone and sang a cappella. Their voices twined and rose in tight harmonies, taking Jake's hopes to the heavens.

How did they know this had been their song? Zora must have told Felicia, which meant that... maybe she was taking this as seriously as he was? He could only hope against hope until he felt like he might break under the weight of it.

The little girls he'd met in her garden, Petra and Vera, exited the multipurpose room and walked across the grass. Their faces were very straight until they walked down the aisle, tossing their rose petals as they grinned. They didn't even bother to try to get the petals onto the ground—they just threw them straight up into the air in big handfuls. The petals whipped in the wind, plastering themselves against cheeks and in hair, making the guests laugh.

He couldn't smile, though. He was too damn scared Zora would change her mind, that she wouldn't show.

Then came Tuesday, followed by Felicia. They

walked so *slowly*. This was agony. How did any man in love ever live through this?

The women stood to his right, on the other side of Norma. The guests turned their heads, watching for Zora to come out the door of the school.

She didn't come.

Jake wondered if he was going to pass out or if his heart would just plain quit beating. If she didn't come, that's for sure what would happen.

"I'm only home in you," the Darling Songbirds sang. It was the last verse.

His eyes were glued on the open door to the multipurpose room.

Tuesday tapped his shoulder. She pointed south, away from the school.

And there she was. Coming out her own gate, walking through the kids' garden. She was barefoot. The wind pushed the dress he'd seen her in at the shop against her body, and she looked like an earth goddess. She carried a single orange dahlia, and he expected flowers to bloom at her feet. Mr. Prickles walked at her ankles as if he were walking her down the aisle. Zora's hair whipped sideways, and her face—

Her face was alight with something he couldn't name. Was it joy? Or radiant fear?

Whatever it was, his own face reflected it, he knew. The rest of the world dropped away. The wind seemed to slow, the music seemed to die, silence filled his ears. Everything was her.

She walked up the aisle, her eyes full of an emotion he was almost too scared to read.

So he whistled. A high *too-whee.*

Zora grinned. She pursed her lips and sent him her upward swooping *whoo-hoot.*

Then she was next to him, her eyes on his. His heart thumped like a freight train on a trestle.

They turned to Norma, who said things. Jake could tell the guests behind him were moved. They sighed and agreed, but he still couldn't make out exactly what she was saying. Not until she asked him to repeat his vows was he able to tune in to the exact words. Hurry, hurry, he had to say it—and then he did. He looked into Zora's eyes, falling into them like they were home. "I do," he said with all his heart.

Zora started to say her vows. Her voice was soft but steady.

And then the hail began to fall.

The hail was as big as gobstoppers, as if dumped from a wheelbarrow above. Guests screamed in laughter and then in actual pain. Most stood and lifted their chairs over their heads. Norma whipped out an umbrella from under her muumuu and held it over Zora, but it turned instantly inside out.

"Here," he said, opening his jacket. "Come here."

She was pressed against him, then, into his body, and his heart finally started beating again as she laughed up into his eyes.

"This is insane!" she yelled, and Jake didn't know what part she was referring to.

The hail got smaller and more painful.

"Oh, no, the garden," she gasped. And she ran.

## THIRTY-FOUR

It didn't matter that she was a runaway bride—she was only running to the other side of the grass. If she could pull the picnic table over the broccoli and kale, there might be a chance for it. By the time she'd run to the edge of the garden, slipping on the icy balls, the tomatoes and lettuce and basil were already done for, but there was still a chance for the hardier plants. Her bare feet skidded in the insta-mud under the mulch. She pulled on the table.

Jake was there, too. He must have been right on her heels. He grabbed the other side. The hail suddenly turned to a downpour, as they dragged the table over the broccoli. When it was in place, she took a moment to look at him.

He was soaked to the skin. His cheeks were flushed, and his hair was flat and dripping.

His smile could have warmed the whole world.

To their left, Petra and Vera were tugging an Adirondack chair. "The sugar peas!" yelled Petra. "They're my favorite!"

Breathlessly, Zora said, "I'll help them. It's probably too late, but can you cover the collards?"

He nodded, and she ran toward the girls. "Thanks for helping! Isn't this weather amazing?"

A loud, electric crack sounded, deeper than a cracking noise should have been. It seemed to come from all around her, and Zora felt everything in her body respond. White heat lit her eyes, and the world disappeared for a split second. She snapped up her head and saw the lightning bolt disappear from the tree it had hit, ripping back into the sky.

The strike had cleaved the trunk of the sycamore. As if it wanted to protect the garden from the hail, the tree seemed to give a curtsy just before it began to fall, slowly— ever so slowly twisting toward them and at the same time so much faster than she could move.

But she *had* to move. She grabbed Vera in one arm and reached for Petra, but she was too far away from her. She wouldn't be able to get them all out of the way, but that didn't change the fact that she *had* to.

Jake was suddenly next to her. He grabbed Petra, whose mouth was open in a silent scream. Zora's bare feet dug into the mud, and she pushed off with all her might. She kept pace with Jake, and as the top half of the tree smashed to earth on top of the garden, just where they'd been, all four of them crashed safely onto the grass.

With everything she had left, Zora reached. She pulled on the huddled form that was Jake covering Petra with his body. Vera's arms stayed clamped so tightly around her neck she could barely breathe. Then the four of them were a clump in the grass, and Jake's hands were brushing the hair out of her eyes. He kissed her, the girls between them, his mouth wet with cold and something warmer. His tears or hers? Did it matter?

Juan Nuñes was there then, and he gathered both of his girls into his arms. He was saying something to them, but Zora couldn't hear him. She didn't need anything but Jake's arms around her. She shivered violently—they both did, she noticed. The hail had stopped, but she was freezing and burning up all at the same time. "Are you okay?"

Jake was saying the same thing against her mouth. "Are you okay? Jesus, are you okay? Are you okay?"

Feet were all around them, and voices exclaimed and shouted. Zora heard her mother's voice, and someone put warm hands on her shoulders.

But only one person got down on the muddy grass with them. Norma, in her yellow robe, plopped down cross-legged and yelled, "Everybody, *shut it!* Okay, sweet peas, we're going to go inside now and get everyone warmed up and dry. But before we do that, is this little ruckus something that you think should stop this wedding? Because we were in the middle of something I feel might be important between you two."

Zora sucked in a breath. They'd almost just died. What kind of a sign was that?

They'd gotten out of it together. Maybe that was all the sign she needed.

Jake spoke, not to Norma, but to her. "These *are* your kids. You love them."

She nodded. "All of them."

"I get it. I see it now. Holy shit, Zora."

And she could tell he did see it. She said, "But *you*. Your boat. *Your* kids."

"I never wanted kids, but I never said it out loud. I just thought a person had to have them when they grew up. I'll be an awesome uncle. And maybe I'll help you with field trips sometimes, if you'll let me."

Zora blinked away more tears as she nodded. "But your trip."

"My roots are here. I know that now. My brothers. My town. And you. Always, only you. It's why I never left." His voice wobbled on the word. "Maybe we'll sail on summer vacations. If you can't, I'll deal with it."

Zora couldn't be away from this man. She didn't want to be away from him for even an hour. Never again. "I've already bought two books on sailing. I learned what a boom vang is."

He grinned so wide it made her own chest expand.

Norma cleared her throat. "Okay, kids, Zora was about to say something. Remember all those vows you made, right before the heavens opened?"

Zora nodded.

"You got a couple of final words for this guy?"

She nodded again, feeling her heart start to bloom. Then she said clearly, "I do."

"Yes! I declare you wife and husband, because screw the patriarchy, you get to go first, Zora. You may kiss your groom!"

A celebratory clap of thunder punctuated the moment her lips touched his with a small electric jolt, a lightning bolt of their own. When she came up for air, a perfect rainbow hung in the sky above their heads. "I love you," she said. "Completely."

"Thank God," he said. "I'll never have to date a stranger on a game show again."

Camille's voice came from above them. "See, honey? I told you that you didn't have to worry about a thing."

"Tuesday," Zora said. "Is your phone in your purse? Is it dry and can I borrow it?"

With the rainbow behind them, as they lay in the muddy grass, her dress and his tux sopping, their hair full of leaves and the odd rose petal, Zora held up the phone and took a selfie of them together. "We'll frame it."

Jake buried his nose in her wet hair. "And put it over the fireplace in a big, fancy frame. You've ruined your dress."

"Yeah, well. I'll never need to wear it again."

"No," Jake said. "You won't."

A great gust of wet air slapped them, and Zora's soaked, muddy hair flew across her face. "Oh!"

Jake kissed her through the dripping mass.

And Zora kissed him right back.

# EPILOGUE

A year later, Zora took a roll of quarters and whacked it against the edge of the wooden table. "See, Petra? It's like cracking an egg, but you hit it harder. Then you hold it over the till drawer and dump them in." She broke the roll in half and the quarters tumbled into their drawer. Around them, the farmer's market swirled—the school's garden stall was right between Scrug Watson's strawberry booth and Lily Dario's tamale stand. The scent of masa and waffle cone filled the air, and a seventies cover band played Fleetwood Mac at the corner. "Now you try it with the pennies."

Petra, who'd shot up two inches over the course of the school year, looked at her seriously. "Harder than breaking an egg."

"Yep." Zora nodded. She didn't realize she should have clarified the instruction until she saw Petra do the windup, her arm over her head. "Not *very* hard—" But it was too late.

Petra slammed the roll's edge against the table. The pennies exploded from their roll, launching themselves into the cucumber pile, the avocado bin, and all over the ground on both sides of the stall.

Petra dropped the empty wrapper and pressed her hands against her mouth. "Oh, *no*. I'm sorry!"

But Zora laughed. "It's just fifty cents. Good arm. Let's see how many we can find."

"But what if we don't find them all?"

Zora winked. "Then we're doing the best thing of all—letting the next person who comes by find a penny for luck."

Three onlookers came to help—of course—and they'd almost found all of the pennies when Zora, reaching around a rack of pamphlets she'd written on organic gardening, heard a voice that still set her heart to racing.

"Damn, you look good in those jeans, Mrs. Ballard."

She straightened, her heart flip-flopping. "Hi, you." Then she registered what Jake was carrying. "Oh!"

His arms were full of dahlias, their orange, red,

and yellow blooms bursting with vibrancy. "Happy anniversary."

*No.* It couldn't be. "That's tomorrow."

"Nope. Today."

She looked at her phone for the date. Crap. She'd ordered a custom-ordered frame made of driftwood crafted by a local artist. She'd hidden it behind the couch. The picture on the mantel of them in the muddy field had been in a plastic Target frame long enough. Damn it. She handed Petra a handful of pennies. "Here, honey, I think that's it. Can you count and see how many we're off by?"

Petra nodded. "And what we lost will be found by other people, so that's good."

"That's *really* good. Thanks for being wonderful." She said it to Petra but looked into Jake's eyes as she did.

He smiled that million-watt smile. "I'll take these home, and then I'll walk back—is Tuesday here to staff the stand?"

"Yeah, she just went to get some horchata."

"Good. I've got another gift to show you."

"Jake." God, she was an *ass.* She hadn't even put the picture in the frame yet.

"Nope. I love that you forgot."

"I forgot our *first.*" She felt terrible.

But he kissed her, a light kiss but one with promise. "I'll be back in ten."

Petra said, "Forty-two cents, Miss Zora."

Zora turned with a smile. "That's perfect. You just made eight people very happy in the future, didn't you?"

Norma arrived at the stand, her aqua muumuu a broad sail. "Hello, my chickens! I need two of your largest zucchinis, please. Don't ask what for, and no matter what you think, I promise, you'd be wrong."

"You got it." There was no way she'd ask.

Ten minutes later, Tuesday was helping Petra bundle basil, and Zora and Jake walked to the marina. It was a perfect midsummer morning—the fog had burned away, and the sun was warm on Zora's bare shoulders.

"I can't wait to show you this," said Jake as he unlocked the dock gate.

"It's nothing expensive, right? I don't need a single thing." Zora had it all already. Him, an amazing job, the perfect home into which Jake fit perfectly. Jake had turned down her offer of putting his name on the deed. *It's always been your home,* he'd said. *It always will be.*

But it wasn't, not really. *Jake* was her home now. They'd sailed to San Diego and back at the beginning of summer. It hadn't been hard, being on the boat for a week and a half, not like she'd thought it would be. It hadn't even been scary. It had been exciting, and nerve-racking at times, because most of the sailing had been done in shipping lanes, so someone had to be awake while they were under sail in order to avoid cargo ships. But they'd been so *together* that when they'd sailed back into Darling Bay, she'd felt almost sad. Home, on that trip, had become the *Kerplunk.*

But most of all, home was Jake's arms.

"Nope," Jake said. "It was practically free."

"*That's* the kind of gift I like." As they approached the boat, she saw that Mallory and Mike were on deck, both looking at their phones. "Hi, guys!"

Mallory flapped a hand at them, and Mike smiled. "Hey! Grill tonight?"

Jake called, "Plans with the brothers tonight. Tomorrow?"

Mallory shot them a thumbs-up and went back to her phone.

Sometime in the last year, Mallory had become a friend, albeit not quite a kindred spirit. The couples grilled dinner together a couple of times a month. Zora found Mike, a banker, *exceedingly* boring, but they were head over heels for each other, so who knew? Love didn't need to make sense. Both couples loved playing poker, and that was enough for an easy friendship between them.

On board, Jake covered her eyes.

Zora smiled. "Is this gift a naked kind of gift? Are we going below deck?"

Jake's voice was a low rumble in her ear that made goosebumps rise on her arms. "That wasn't in the plan, but…"

"Because I can think of several anniversary gifts I could give to you down there. I have a couple that you'll need to unwrap quite carefully." Of course, the truth was that they were gifts to herself, too.

Keeping her eyes covered with his hands, Jake kissed her neck with a growl. "Move forward, woman, before I make you walk the plank."

Two steps, then three to the right. Then, right where she figured the edge of the ladder should be, he stopped her.

"Okay."

But he didn't remove his hands. She lifted her own to touch the backs of his wrists. "Are you going to show me?"

"I'm suddenly nervous I did it wrong."

"I bet you didn't."

"Or you won't like it."

"I bet I will." Whatever it was, he'd thought of her. She'd love it.

"Okay." He removed his hands.

And there, at her feet, was a tiny garden, less than two feet long and maybe six inches wide. The plants were in a low box set flush along the rail. Lettuce, and rosemary, and basil, and a fruiting cherry tomato plant. There were chives and arugula and cilantro.

Zora's heart grew so big it barely fit in her chest. "Where did you get these?" She knew that tomato, she *knew* she did.

"Tuesday might have helped me pull the plants up from the garden school. You had so many, though, I thought it would be okay to take some."

Her smile was so big it hurt her face. "Are you kidding? It's wonderful."

"And the soil is from the garden, too."

She *got* it then. Breathlessly, she said, "So we take home with us when we sail."

Jake nodded, his eyes bright. "Look, this is the soil catcher. I lined it with coffee filters, so no dirt will wash out onto the deck. I made a lid, here. So if waves are high, salt water won't splash in. And this clear plastic guard should protect it from most spray while also acting as a kind of tiny greenhouse."

She turned away from the plants and wrapped her arms around his waist. Her throat was tight. "This is the nicest present anyone's ever given me. Our plants, our soil."

"Our soil for our sail," he said.

They were headed to Hawaii. It would take almost three weeks of open water to get there. Then she'd fly home for the start of school, and Jake would bring the boat back on his own. That part—knowing he'd be alone out there—terrified her. They'd added the widow's walk to the top of the cottage, but she'd said she'd only look at the ocean when he was there to look with her.

But their leg of the journey? Zora couldn't believe how much she was looking forward to it, to being with him that whole time on the ocean which she'd grown to love. They sailed every weekend and surfed at least once a month, and Zora had started taking scuba lessons on her own—something that Jake wasn't very interested in.

"Thank you," she said to him. She rested her head against his chest for a moment, listening for the solid thumping that told her he was there with her. He was *right* there with her, his wide hands strong on the small of her back. The boat rocked under their feet, but Zora had her sea legs, and more—she had him to brace herself against as she provided bracing for him.

"We're home," Jake said. It was what he always said, whether they were in the cottage or in the berth below. He said it into her hair in the middle of the night, and he said it when she kissed him goodbye in the morning.

Joy rose inside Zora's chest, bubbles made of hope and happiness and love. She felt her roots twine around his and go through the boat's deck, down through the hull, through the water and into the sand below. Then she lifted her lips to his and said against his mouth, "We're home, my love."

The End

# DEAR READER

Dear Reader,

There's nothing I love more than when I finish reading a book and heave that happy sigh of contentedness. The main characters are in love. Everything has worked out. The kiss is passionate, and I can almost *feel* those lips on mine.

You've got that feeling right now, don't you? Yeah, I *totally* want to be out on Jake's boat with him, too. I want Zora's garden (mine is full of weeds because I spend so much time writing!).

What I *hate* is when I have to crawl out from under my covers and get up and do laundry or make dinner. Screw cleaning the coffee pot. I want to keep dreaming these sweet, sexy dreams.

So sometimes I just keep reading. Maybe you

do, too. You should try the first book in the Darling Songbird series, which starts on the next page. The favorite series of *many* of my readers, I get emails about the Darling sisters almost every day. Here's a sneak peek at Adele, arriving in town to find nothing but an old bar and a guy so hot she can barely look at him. And just like Jake and Zora, they have a history neither can forget.

Enjoy.

Love,

Rachael

# The Darling Songbirds

# THE DARLING SONGBIRDS

The saloon had always looked old-fashioned, but now it resembled a set in a ghost town. The boards creaked under Adele Darling's feet as if they hadn't been stepped on since women wore hoop skirts. Cobwebs on the porch slung themselves from top beams to bottom ones, and an old wagon wheel leaned against a hitching post in front. It was as if the sidewalk had been poured right around the post, and her Toyota hybrid looked completely wrong parked next to it. It should have been a horse.

The problem was that Adele wasn't in an old western, or a ghost town. Darling Bay was the sleepy gold-rush town her great-grandfather had given his name to.

The town she'd left for good a long time ago.

There was a hand-drawn sign that said: *Hours –
11 AM–2 AM*. She glanced at her cell phone. Almost noon, and the doors were locked. Awesome.

She knocked on the wood next to the iron
screen door.

"That won't do you no good."

Adele spun. "Sorry?"

The exceedingly short woman standing on the
step below her wore a long, oversized blue dress
that hung on her like a sack. Somewhere in her mid-sixties, she had a well-creased face, like a crumpled
envelope. A dozen or more necklaces dangled
around her neck, crystals and quartz and what
looked like actual feathers, on tarnished silver
chains. Her short grey hair stuck up in spikes as if
she'd just run her hands over it roughly, but her
smile was wide. "He ain't here yet."

Adele wasn't sure who *he* was. "Okay . . ."

"But if you reach up above the door," the
woman pointed, "yeah, right there. You're a tall one,
ain't you? Grab that key for us, will you?"

It wasn't that Adele was tall at five foot five. It
was more like the woman was eye level to her elbow. "Got it." Now that the key was in her hand,
Adele had no idea what to do with it. It wasn't like
she would just unlock the bar's front door.
Would she?

She didn't have to make the decision. In a move

so quick it surprised her, the woman snatched the key from her palm and unlocked the iron security door, swinging it wide open and barreling through the wooden half-door as if she owned the place, which Adele knew for a fact she didn't.

"Sometimes I gotta open up for him, you know?" The woman moved to the right and snapped on two light switches, and then headed for the bar. She was a low, fast-moving bowling ball in blue. "It's usually harder 'cause it's tough for me to reach that key. It's not like I mess with the till or nothin', I just help him out where I can."

Adele trailed behind the woman. This wasn't the situation she had imagined herself in when she'd awoken this morning. All she'd known four hours ago in her San Francisco hotel was that she had a long drive up the coast. When she got to Darling Bay, she figured she would plan her next move.

So she'd gotten in her rental car and headed north. Highway One wound through the redwoods, darting out to the rocky coast and back inland again. She'd stopped once to stretch her legs, and had stood cliff-side watching elephant seals slap themselves up and down the coarse sand. It took a bit more than three hours to get to Darling Bay, a long-enough drive to make her feel as far from Nashville as she'd ever felt.

She used to be used to this feeling. This used to be home.

And now she had exactly no idea what that meant.

"You want a drink, dearie?"

Adele blinked. "I'm sorry . . . Who are you?"

"Well, I suppose I could ask you the same thing."

That was fair. "I'm Adele Darling."

"Oh, my *God*. You *are*."

Crap. Adele should have just said her first name. What was she thinking? Nowhere else would her last name have raised more than a vaguely puzzled eyebrow. *Sounds familiar . . . can't place it.* But not here.

The woman clutched at her pile of necklaces. "They didn't tell me that."

"Who?" Adele was feeling more confused by the second. "I don't think anyone knew I was coming."

"But they usually tell me everything." She held up a chain that had a pink piece of stone at the end and peered at it closely.

"Your necklaces tell you these things?" Adele kept her voice soft. Maybe it was better not to startle her.

The woman stared at Adele as if she were crazy. "Not my necklaces. My *dreams*."

"Ah."

"Of course, it's not like they're always right. Sometimes they tell me a storm is coming when all that's going to happen is I forget to take the kettle off the stove. Same thing." She waved her arms above her head. "Clouds of steam. Just in my kitchen. You see?"

Adele nodded carefully.

"Where are the other two?" The woman peered behind Adele as if she were somehow hiding her sisters.

"Not with me." Nothing could be truer. "I didn't get your name." Adele held out her hand.

The woman's shake was firm. "Norma."

"And you're the bartender?"

Norma laughed heartily, but she spread her palms on the top of the bar as if to negate her next statement. "Oh no, not me. You're a funny one. I'm just a drinker, from a long line of the same. Speaking of which, what can I make you?"

Not the bartender, then, but not *not* the bartender. "How about a Coke?"

"With rum? And can I read your tarot cards?" Norma asked hopefully.

"I'm good on both, thanks." It was a bit early to start pounding liquor. "So if you're not the bartender, and the saloon was supposed to open at eleven . . ."

"Oh, he'll be here."

"Who will?" This was beginning to feel like a game of Who's On First.

"Nate."

"Nate?"

"You don't know him?"

"I haven't been here in a while," Adele said. If a while meant eleven years. She'd been far away from Darling Bay, sometimes as far as a person could get. "*When* do you think he'll be here?"

Norma frowned and held one of her necklaces, looking upward as if the answer hung in the cobwebbed rafters. "Soon." Then she filled a glass with Coke and slid it towards Adele. "Here you go. Now, tell me everything. How're your sisters? You know, my dad – may he rest in peace – died before y'all got famous, but I always think he would have loved you. When *your* dad died, I asked my dad to bring him into heaven with a big ol' hug. Felt so bad for you young gals. Are you getting the band back together? You know we talk about you all the time. And those magazines, they stopped printing those stories about y'all, and that's a good thing, but we never believed a word they said anyway. How's the little one? Lana?"

The back of Adele's throat itched. "Fine." She had no idea how Lana was since she never answered Adele's phone calls. The ache of it was dull and familiar. "Do you mind if I have a look around? While I wait for Nate?"

"Sure, sure." Norma bobbed up and down behind the bar, spinning into action. Tomato juice, sliced celery, vodka. "A Bloody Mary doesn't just appear out of nowhere. Gotta work at it." She frowned and looked upward again. "Unless you stare into the mirror, you know? And say those words? I'm not gonna do *that*. Okay. There." She added a dash of Tabasco. "Mine isn't as good as Nate's, but I'm getting there. Just gotta keep working on it."

Adele wandered towards the rear of the saloon. It was just as she remembered it, dark and dusty, smelling of splintered wood and spilled beer. The old jukebox glowed neon blue and green in the far right corner. Next to it was a skinny ATM that had been added since she was last here. To the left of that ran the long bar all the way to the back wall. How many buckets of ice had Adele hauled out of the old storeroom? The girls had loved being there in the saloon, still under-age, helping Uncle Hugh with stocking and refilling in the afternoons. They'd begged to be allowed to stay as late as they could, listening to the music, not leaving until Sheriff Tate came in after his shift and raised his eyebrows at the little girls doing their homework in the far left corner on the big, scarred wooden table.

The table was still there. Adele touched the top of it, feeling the ridges with her fingertips. People still carved their initials into it, using penknives and ballpoint pens. They didn't cut deeply (out of respect, perhaps – surely they would have dug more deeply into a tree) and the well-worn initials looped over each other, years and years of couples who had loved and lost and loved again. When Adele and her sisters had done their math homework here, they'd had to make sure their notepads were under their papers, or their pencils would stab through into the table's scars.

Somewhere on the table were their initials, too. All three of them, *AD + MD + LD. Adele and Molly and Lana.* Hidden now somewhere, buried by the map of other letters.

Adele realized she was humming and closed her throat. She heard the refrain of "You'll Never Leave" in her mind. Then she wandered back towards the front door. To the right was the stage. Just a couple of feet higher than the floor, it was made of the same old wood and, if she remembered right, just as rickety. Impulsively, she jumped up onto it, stretching her arms wide. A light snapped on above her head, and she grinned in delight. Even when they were kids, Uncle Hugh had kept that motion-activated light there, and they'd loved the way it had shone down on them like a spotlight.

"Sing us a song!" called Norma from the other side of the saloon.

*Oh, hell, no.* Adele swallowed her grin and raised a hand. "Maybe later." Or maybe never.

The old pool table stood in the same spot it always had. Adele could imagine a tsunami sweeping in and taking out the Golden Spike, carrying away the saloon and the café and the old hotel – the whole town of Darling Bay itself – but that pool table, as heavy as sin and older than Eve's apple, would stay right there, right where it had always been meant to sit. At some point over the years, the felt playing top had been repaired. Chalks, the old square kind, were lined up on the rail, and a half-dozen cue sticks leaned drunkenly against the short inner wall.

Adele could almost hear the crack of the balls. Molly had been their ringer, always willing to bat her eyes innocently at whatever guy thought it would be fun to show off his pool prowess to teenage girls. Molly would run the table, stick the guy's money in her pocket, and then ask Uncle Hugh for a round of root beer floats for her and her sisters.

Molly. She wanted Molly here.

She pulled out her cell phone. *Remember the root beer floats?*

Holding her phone in her hand in case the text

actually managed to soar out to the cruise ship somewhere on the ocean, Adele used her other hand to lift up the bench seat in the front window alcove. There they were, all the board games they'd spent so much time with. She'd be willing to bet that the Monopoly set was still missing all the Get Out of Jail Free cards. (Sheriff Tate had gotten his feelings hurt one night when he'd been on a particularly expensive Monopoly losing streak.) And the Sorry! game . . . She pulled it out and lifted the lid. Yep, there they were. Each piece had little teeth marks at the top, marching all the way around. The blue piece was missing the round knobby top altogether.

While Adele raced around the board, passing her sisters with a cheery "Sorry!" Lana would get so mad she'd chew the pieces, leaving her tooth marks behind, or in the case of the blue one, biting the top right off.

Adele glanced left. Norma was looking into her Bloody Mary as if it were telling a fortune, so Adele quietly slipped the headless blue piece into her jeans pocket. From the layers of dust inside the bench seat, no one would miss the piece anytime soon.

She looked out the side alcove window. Across the middle parking lot stood the old café. Funny, she'd assumed it would still be open, that Hugh's employees would still be running it. But it was shuttered and dark, an unbearable sense of loneliness coming from the ripped awning. The old caboose that had been a coffee stand rusted in front, near the sidewalk. She looked right, up to the slight rise behind the saloon and café. That was the hotel, the third old building that she'd called home every summer of her youth. It was where she would sleep tonight. She yearned for that, for this already-long day to speed up until she could just lie down, close her eyes, and breathe in the ocean-scented air.

The phone – the real one that hung on the bar's back wall – jangled. Adele jumped. Norma grabbed it without hesitation. "Golden Spike, this is Norma!"

There was a pause. "Yeah." She grinned. "Right again. You bet. I'll keep 'er running, boss. Yeah. Okay. And hey? I forgot to tell you I need a raise." She slammed the phone down with a hoot of laughter. "That was him!" She looked at Adele as if suddenly surprised to see her. "Oh! I should have told him you were here."

"No, that's okay. I'll see him when he gets here."

"So I guess *you're* the boss around here now." Norma was obviously startled by the thought, her grey eyebrows shooting higher. "Of course you are. Oooh." Her drink wrapped tightly in her hand, she leaned forward from her bar stool. "You should tell him to hire me. I wouldn't drink all the booze, I *swear* I wouldn't." But there was a twinkle behind her expression that said the opposite was true, and that they both knew it.

Nate shouldn't have answered his cell phone that morning, but he was a sucker for a blonde. Especially if the blonde happened to be ninety-one and living on the boat he'd sold her five months earlier. Ruthann Suthers had asked, "Does it matter, dear, if my extension cord in the kitchen smokes a little?" Nate thought of the electrical fire at the hotel, and told her to call 911. She said, "I already did. They said it was okay, but they shut off my power." Nate had sighed and spent the next two hours crawling around the baseboards in the boat's mess. He'd installed three new surge protectors, and he'd tested each outlet. By the time he'd finished, he'd bruised a knuckle and ripped his favorite Merle Haggard T-shirt.

And he was late.

At least Norma had been at the bar to open up. Unless a wandering tourist or two showed up, she'd probably be the only customer until three, anyway.

He parked his truck in front of the post office. Getting out, he pulled his Charlie's Feed and Seed ball cap on backward. What he really needed was another shower. Maybe he could bribe Norma with a couple more drinks off her tab to stay a little longer while he cleaned up. He took the two shallow steps up off street level with one long jump.

Inside the saloon it was dim compared to the bright morning sunlight. Norma grinned at him from her regular bar stool. "Boss!"

"You keeping out the riffraff?" Too late, he noticed that someone else *was* in the saloon, way over by the bench full of board games. "Whoops." Not even a tourist – a pretty tourist, at that – wanted to be called riffraff.

"Nah, they're getting in. And hey, guess who it is."

He looked again. The woman was standing straighter now, pretending not to hear them. She kept her eyes out the side alcove window as if there was something more than just the old, closed Golden Spike Café across the parking lot to look at. And she wasn't just pretty. From this angle, she was a sight closer to beautiful. God, who did she remind him of? She must have driven up from the city or something. Some model, waiting for her photographer to shoot her on the beach. He'd seen it plenty of times before, pretty girls thinking it would be good to get shots of themselves in the water, or leaning against the high cliffs down at Fenton's Cove, not realizing that the fog bank usually made it not only a shoot in bad light, but also a shoot where they'd freeze their dang nipples off. If they stayed till October, maybe. That's when the sun came out around here, after the summer tourists had given up all hope and left. But this woman, with her honeyed hair and that perfect long nose, those lips that were quirking into something that looked like it was close to a smile, she'd be shivering in her two-piece soon enough.

"Howdy," he said politely. If his ball cap had been forward-facing, he would have touched the brim, but as it was he left his arms at his sides.

She turned to face him, and in that motion his heart dropped to the old floorboards and went right through, straight down to the dust and packed earth below, not stopping until it hit the world's molten core.

Adele Darling. Out of freaking *nowhere*.

KEEP READING - Available wherever you buy books!

# ABOUT RACHAEL

**Rachael Herron** is the internationally best-selling author of more than twenty books, including thriller (under R.H. Herron), mainstream fiction, feminist romance, memoir, and nonfiction about writing. She received her MFA in writing from Mills College, Oakland, and she teaches writing extension workshops at both UC Berkeley and Stanford. She is a proud member of the NaNoWriMo Writer's Board. She's a New Zealand citizen as well as an American.

She'd love to hear from you!
Facebook | Twitter | Blog | Patreon